# A gentle soul

## Marian Flowers

# Contents

# Chapter 1

Every single day, Dove's classmates are irritated by the sound of her acrylic white nails striking the laptop keys. They find her to be distracting, thus they dread seeing her enter the classroom. for a variety of reasons. It's difficult for others behind her to see her because of the bun she wears her shoulder-length locs in. She chews with her mouth shut even if it makes her nervous. What then is the issue?

As far as she's aware, there's no issue. merely because they avoid her. Despite the fact that she is the sweetest person any of them have ever met, her presence terrifies them. All of them want to get out of the way because of the way she walks. It's all in the way she speaks; her voice carries authority, and her smile could convince you of anything.

However, the entire school would follow in her wake as she sang. Only if they were aware of her abilities.

"Dov- " He was about to say anything when Dove blew a bubble, prompting him to moan. Even her professors weren't really fond of her.

She was concentrated because she knew that finishing the sixty-page report wouldn't just happen. Because polar ice was her favourite flavour and she had just purchased a new pack of gum last night, chewing gum also helped her concentrate. She was going to be functional for the remainder of the week.

Say "Dove Dasani!" Mr. Willcox shouted and hit the metal desk with his palm. That will leave a mark.

As she took out the airpods from her ears and listened to the song Fantasia - Lose to Win, Dove's gaze first shifted to his hand next to her laptop, then up to his eyes. Yes, you are required in the admissions office. He interrupted her, obviously irritated. He thought she was problematic. He believed she scarcely paid attention to his lectures because she was always off in her own world, but he was mistaken. similarly to her other professors.

Dove is incredibly perceptive. Whether others believe it or not, she listens to everything, and her eyes see a lot that others don't.

She nodded, and he backed away from the desk while murmuring things that she overheard him think she hadn't. She simply didn't want to respond.

She left the room and immediately headed for the office. which is a few of halls away.

A few others gave her sidelong glances as she walked, and when she gave them a tiny grin and a courteous wave, they did the same for her.

When she finally arrived at the office door, she shifted her weight and gave it a gentle knock. I said, "Come on in!" She entered after hearing Principal Grint's friendly voice instruct her to do so.

"Hold on a second." Sitting in the leather chair in front of her oak wood desk, she told the newcomer to the school. She gave Dove a hearty hug. "How are you doing?" Dove answered by assuming nothing. "Okay, so you needed me?" The teacher inquired, and the teacher nodded.

"Kareem here," He turned around as he heard her point to the male occupying the seat. He stood as the teacher signalled for him to do so, tugging his jeans up only for them to drop back down.

She wasn't particularly skilled at interacting with strangers, but Dove had an excellent way of masking it. "Hello." She extended her hand and smiled warmly as she greeted him. His other hand was clutching his slacks, so he took a moment to glance down at her hand before shaking it with the free one. "Wassup." She continued to smile and retrieved her hand as he nodded his head.

Kareem recently transferred here, so I was wondering if you could show him around since his classes don't start till next week. You have all the time you need. It would be greatly appreciated. With a smile of optimism, the idea expressed.

Dove is a great student, she is aware of this. She also understood how good it would be for Kareem to be shown about by a kind and patient person.

Yes, I won't mind. Should I begin today? Dove questioned, hesitant to return to Mr. Willcox's class. He needs to go to a meeting, but you too can decide when you'll give him the tour. The principal spoke fast as she seized the file containing Kareem's personal data.

Dove nodded and then turned to face Karrem, who was contemplating something. His siblings and grandparents were constantly on his mind. He let out a sigh as he gazed out the window at the crowded student courtyard. He has a task to finish and a person to make happy.

The words of his grandma kept repeating in his head. "You have a second opportunity, but not everyone does. Make it count and be proud of me. He nodded when she caressed his cheek and turned to hug his brothers as she continued. "Bye, Reem!" He grabbed onto their bodies, grinning as they yelled.

"Kareem?" Once more, Dove's cry jolted him out of his reverie. I'm sorry, what did you say? She was the focus of his question.

Dove repeated herself while grinning. "There's a McDonald's at the entrance to this hall, so I thought we could meet there tomorrow morning and start the tour."

Kareem gave a nod. Cool, and thank you for your agreement, by the way. He talked openly. He had spent the entire morning sitting in this office, and many employees had declined to show him around. Due to his appearance, he was aware of the reason. Men with dark skin and dark hair. His kinky hair was flowing freely, and he had tattoos, piercings, and drooping jeans. He was prepared to go somewhere and pass out, so he didn't really care what other people thought.

He was unable to accomplish that because he was now attending a meeting to discuss his behaviour and the number of strikes still remaining on his registered hands.

Dove waved her hand, showing that she was happy to assist. She had experienced what it was like to be the new kid—and the new black kid. She and approximately eleven other black students out of the thousands of students who attend Mentone University are a result of this school's relative youth.

"Don't bring it up. But what do you require right now? I mean, is everything okay? He shrugged in response to her query. "Meeting." She remembered when he reminded her, and she nodded. Well, have a wonderful day, but hold on. Pulling her phone out, she broke off. "Would you mind exchanging phone numbers?" When she enquired, he took out his phone. "Naw." He responded, and then they exchanged phone numbers before parting ways.

"Thanks, Dove!" Dove smiled and waved back before turning around and walking down the corridor while Principle Grint yelled and waved her hand.

<h1 align="right">Chapter 2</h1>

Dove entered the main hall while tightly encircling the light brown jumper she was wearing on top of her plain white shirt. She didn't anticipate it being this cold today. As she entered the building and stepped on the tile floor, the heel of her footwear clanked.

"I'm so sorry," While looking around, she apologised and grabbed the glass door that she almost dropped. She was a little bit late, so she wasn't sure if Kareem was present. "Thanks." Kareem thanked her and entered the structure.

Who are you searching for? He looked around and questioned. Dove re-wrapped her arms around the jumper as she opened the door. You might not recognise this man, but I'm looking for him. She continued to gaze around before swiftly turning to her left, looking away, and then gazing back. "Kareem!" He laughed as he observed her surprised expression as she yelled.

That surprised her because, according to her typical abilities, she failed to detect that he was standing next to her. Happy morning. She smiled and nodded as he welcomed her. Happy morning. She responded and then let her hands hang. Would you like to dine here, or should we go to the dining hall? Not really knowing what to say or do, she made a suggestion.

Kareem gave it some thinking. Has the dining hall added more restaurants? When he inquired, Dove nodded. "I would also suggest building your own waffle station. Easy and beneficial. Kareem nodded as Dove continued.

"Set the example." Turning around, he murmured, holding open the door for her. He followed her outside the door while tucking his hands into the pocket of his grey Nike jogging pants. She sent him a quick thank you before leaving.

They started moving towards the dining room by moving down the courtyard. "So, here." Kareem glanced to his right at the enormous, aging-looking structure as Dove pointed to the library. Since the library is a common facility, anyone who isn't a student or a member of the school community is welcome to visit it. Kareem noticed a smaller, more recent-looking building as she pointed once more. Is a private library that is only available to Mentone University faculty and students. He nodded as she continued. So anyone who choose not to travel there can simply visit the campus and go up there? Kareem enquired while indicating the neighbourhood library.

Avian nodded. "Yes, I believe it to be risky, but I must admit that the campus security is excellent. The campus security office is there. She pointed, and he turned to gaze at the area, which resembled a miniature version of a police station. "Cool." She gave him a little smile as she nodded in agreement.

The dining room was now just a short distance away for them. "You see those two connected buildings there?" Kareem looked at the connected structure as Dove questioned him. That is the space for electives or activities and the health centre. Dove replied as she relaxed her arm.

"Like the gym and f*cking shit?" She affirmed when Kareem asked. "Yep. I think it's great that they placed the medical facility close by in case of injury. Dove muttered, putting her thumbs in the pockets of her jeans.

"Do you engage in any sport, dance, or activity like that?" She shook her head as she looked down at her footwear and he inquired. "Nah." Lowly, she said. It's true that she doesn't dance or do any sports. She has always had music on the brain. since she was a young child.

Her third insecurity out of three was simply that she didn't feel comfortable with others knowing that she sang. Although she strives to love herself, there are still instances when she doesn't.

Do you engage in any athletic activity? To divert attention from herself, she asked. Kareem gave a nod. "I play baseball and run track." He commented after observing her altered mood.

Kareem is watchful, much like Dove. Will you run and play for the school? When she inquired, he shrugged. "I'm going to set myself up first, I don't know yet. Den, I'll choose. She once again encircled the jumper with her arms as she nodded in response to his words. She regretted not dressing in anything warmer.

To allow Dove to enter, Kareem opened the glass door by grabbing it and stepping to the side. He could sense her coldness. "Thanks." She entered the heated, packed building after thanking him.

So, what do you want to eat? She enquired as she observed all the nearby restaurants. Get some donuts, please. Kareem pointed to the tiny Dunkin Donuts section and stated. Dove smiled while nodding.

Before they could get to the checkout, they briefly stood in the queue. "Welcome to Dunkin. How may I help you?" Freshman asked, and they both perused the menu together. "Please wait a moment." Kareem muttered, unsure of which donut he preferred.

You are aware of what you want. Dove was just considering what she wanted when he asked, and she nodded. "I chose a regular iced coffee and an egg and ham English muffin." He nodded as she continued to study the menu. You all ready? Kareem nodded as he was requested by the freshman. "Lemme get two egg muff-- watchu say?" Dove laughed as he questioned her. You receiving what I'm receiving? He nodded and grinned a little as she questioned. "Ok." To the girl, she turned. "Can we please have two iced coffees and two egg and ham English muffins?" Vee enquired. and the freshmen tapped out their orders while nodding.

The time is "that'll be thirteen twenty eight." The student said while grinning at what she believed to be a pair.

Dove extended the cash to her; Kareem screwed his face, seized her arm, and she stared at him bewildered. No offence meant, but move. He was serious when he spoke, and Dove laughed before realising he was serious. "Ok.." She let her hand hang and muttered.

At most, she was mildly astonished. She was rather shocked. Except when she was on a date or it was her parents, she wasn't used to someone buying or paying for her; even in those two circumstances, she preferred to make her own purchases.

After giving the first-year student a twenty dollar cash and giving him his change, Kareem turned to Dove and laughed. "Calm down." She grinned a little as he touched her shoulder. "Thanks." He waved his hand in response to her thanks. "Jus me." As he seized their possessions, he stated while shrugging.

"What do you mean?" She enquired as she followed him to a two-person unoccupied table. Das is just who I am. She was seated across from him and nodded as he rephrased. Just know that I'll pay next time. She said, taking a straw and her drink. Kareem raised an eyebrow and grinned. "When next?" She was sipping her drink when he asked, and her eyes widened. I meant to say that, but never mind. She spoke humbly, her head shaking.

In such a short period of time, she discovered that she was enjoying his company; it felt different to her. She doesn't get along with anyone at Mentone University because they don't get along with her, and she's never been friends with a guy who wasn't continually making advances towards her or attempting to hit then dip.

It wouldn't bother me to chill witchu. She raised her eyebrows as Kareem shrugged. The question "For real?" After asking, she dug into her sandwich. He gave a nod. Don't act startled, you're in excellent company. Before taking a bite of his meal, he said. She wanted to express her gratitude, but her mouth was full of food, so instead she simply grinned and held up her thumb. Given that he also had food in his mouth, he held his hand up to his lips and hummed while laughing.

She spoke differently from the girls back home, and Kareem found her alluring because of the way she held herself. Since he doesn't know anyone else, he wouldn't mind spending more time with her.

# Chapter 3

---

Dove picked up the freshly purchased box of cheerios from the top of her little fridge and set it down on her wooden desk. When she went shopping, Walmart was out of reese's puffs, which she really wanted. She began to pour the cereal into the bowl after she had opened the box and the plastic bag, but she stopped as her phone began to ring.

After setting the box next to the bowl, she went to her bed, sat down, and took the call while picking up the phone. "Heyo!" She greeted, and Kareem grinned at the phone before turning to the offered laptop by the school.

He merely brought himself and his clothes, not much else. Nothing additional, as he didn't have much extra to pack. Was-sup, what are you doing? He enquired after selecting the Jesse Owens story. "Truthfullyyyy." He arched an eyebrow as he waited to see what she would say as she dragged. "I'm putting things off. locating anything to do aside from this assignment.

When she talked candidly, Kareem shook his head and turned to face the phone.

"Why are you doing your job? You must be there. Knowing how quickly you may fall behind by skipping one task, he said. Dove is a brilliant girl, thus there is no reason why she should be failing, as he could also see. She replied, "I know, but I just don't want to do it," and he kept shaking his head. "Watchu majoring again?" He questioned as he returned his focus to his task. "Criminal Justice is a terrific subject, I mean that. Simply said, it's not what I desire. She whispered the final sentence, and he nodded without hearing her.

Dove wouldn't have chosen criminal justice, but given the circumstances, it is what was decided for her. With both of her parents employed in the field, it was only natural for them to want their young daughter to follow in their footsteps. They continually minimised her participation and insisted she need-ed something steady that would take off right away, despite the fact that she had repeatedly stated her desire to major in music performance.

Additionally, they didn't believe she could sing, which caused her early vocal insecurity.

Are you majoring in sports management or sports history? Dove questioned because she no longer wanted to be the cen-tre of attention. While typing, Kareem nodded. He is aware that he called her, but he didn't really speak. She will, however, soon have his whole attention because he will have finished writing the Jesse Owens report he was given earlier. He needed to make this year count, so he will.

He had just been released from prison when he received an academic scholarship to attend Mentone University. Kareem never anticipated finding himself in jail, but events conspired to get him there. Fortunately, the judge before whom he appeared knew of his grandmother and was able to use his connections to ensure that Kareem's record would be clear other from his registered hands.

He will make the most of the opportunity and take excellent care of himself and his family. His second chance is definitely a blessing.

He grinned as he submitted the task and then returned his attention to the phone. Dove is so lovely. He observed her eating the dry cheerios while she was engrossed in the Boy Meets World offshoot Girl Meets World on television. You ought to let your hair down more. Nodding in agreement with himself, he said. Dove almost caused herself whiplash as she rapidly glanced to her right at the phone resting on the cushion. "What do you say?" Kareem laughed as she questioned while consuming more porridge. She always seemed as though she was shocked whenever he complimented her or said anything good to her.

You're really attractive, right? Dove remained silent as she regarded the phone while he inquired, raising his eyebrows. "I-- thanks." Before turning back to her preferred television programme, she murmured. "Don't be a wimpy shawty," Kareem continued to smile as he spoke, and the redness on her high, yellow cheeks made his smile even more brilliant.

Dove couldn't believe the compliments she was receiving from this great ass dude. Any black man she attempted to even be friends with rejected her on the grounds that she was too white, and this gorgeous chocolate man at that.

It was strange when Kareem complimented her; she wanted to urge him to stop talking and hang up, but she also wanted to tell him to go on. She was unsure of both her feelings and what to say.

"Dove." Kareem dialled her number simply to annoy her after realising his effect. To him, it was sweet yet rather depressing. It proved to him that she wasn't frequently complimented. "Yes, Kareem?" Dove questioned since she was aware of what he was doing and saw that he wasn't cunning. I believe you are. You are special in some way. When Dove saw him get up from his seat and start singing while snapping his fingers, she grinned. "I bring you along on a shopping trip. Because I love you so much. She laughed as he started doing the dougie while still singing and pointing at the phone.

"Ayyyy!" As he began performing the dolphin dance he had seen on Tiktok, she gassed him. As he took his seat, he chuckled and shook his head. Except for his siblings and pals from home, he had never been so silly around or with anybody else. whom he had long known.

Dove interrupted the screen capture, caused him to slap his lips, and she burst out laughing. You no longer have access to facetime with me for the remainder of the week, as you can see. Her smile faded at his quip. "Are you serious?" When she inquired, he started to chuckle as well.

# Chapter 4

------------------------------------------------

"**D**amn shawty!" Kareem hissed, and Dove chuckled. "My bad, this the last braid." She assured him, knowing she had three more to go. He lifted his hand to see if she was lying and she stopped braiding to swat it away. "Ian lying." She told him, quietly laughing but he of course heard her. "Da lord gone strike you fa lying." Kareem said, trying to nod his head but he couldnt even move without it hurting and Dove couldnt help but laugh louder.

After the final few braids Dove grabbed the the mirror from beside her and passed it to Kareem allowing him to see the pop smoke braids. "You did yo shit foreal." He said, smiling in the mirror and she smiled too.

"Thank you." She thanked him, tapping his shoulder and he stood up from the rolling chair allowing her to push it back and get off her bed. "Watchu said you wanted to eat?" He asked, knowing she was just as hungry as him.

"Um...ion know. You decide." She told him, pulling her phone out of her back pocket. It had been going off the whole time she was doing his hair.

He nodded. "Imma just get some stuff from Mcdonalds, unless you wanna order some." He shrugged, not really caring. As long as he ate.

"Ill order that cajun pasta stuff from Friday's." She said, going to the message's app on her phone. "Das da shit we had few weeks ago?" He asked, laying back on her bed and Dove nodded. "Yea." she replied, sitting beside him.

Clicking on her mother's contact she sighed reading the long message about the importance of her replying to any text sent from her parents. Dove understood that her momma means well, but this isnt the only thing she lectures her about. She could do the littlest thing and Tasha would find a way to make the situation bigger.

All she wanted to do was make them proud, even when it wasnt something she wanted. Anything for her parents.

"Was wrong?" Kareem asked, observing her deflated expression and body language. "Huh- oh im good." She replied, clicking off the message and going to her contacts to call the Friday's restaurant.

"So were doing the caju- Ay no disrespect but ion like dat." Kareem cut her off, sitting up and she looked at him confused. "You dont like the pasta?" She asked and he shook his head. "Ion like da fact dat you push all yo emotions unda da rug like dey dont matta, or if you got some to say you wont say it. Stop doing dat. Your feelings matter just like anybody elses." He said, looking into her eyes and she slowly nodded.

"Say whatchu mean and mean watchu say. Got me?" He asked, with a smile causing her to smile. "I gotchu." She replied and he raised an eyebrow. "Look atchu sounding black." He joked, and she pushed his shoulder while rolling her eyes.

He chuckled, grabbing the roku television remote. "What you about to put on?" She asked, placing her dinging phone beside her. She wasnt for the drama her mother was bringing, so she was just gonna enjoy her time with Kareem being that they both have busy weeks coming up.

He looked from her phone to her and she shoved it under the pillow, acting like she didnt feel him looking. He sighed, shaking his head. "Boys in da hood." He replied and she raised her eyebrow's. "Whats dat bout?" She asked and he smirked, looking at her and she knew exactly what he was going to say.

"You want me ta say it?" He asked, still smirking and she sighed. "Gone head." She said, shaking her head. "I mean its pretty self explanatory, the title is boys in da hood." He said, mocking her whenver he'd ask a question where the answer was obvious. "I dont even sound like that, so boom." She said, rolling her neck and doing the grasp hand motion.

"Oh shit, you getting ta be ratchet." He joked and the two laughed. "Its gonna be your fault, you have me watching all these movies." She said, smiling and his eyes grew big.

"Gonna?" He said, in soulja boy's voice and they started laughing again.

# Chapter 5

------------------------------------------------------------

Kareem pulled his jeans up as he walked down the hall, towards the office. He yawned reaching the door. It's a early morning, the principle said he was needed as soon as possible. After a few knocks the door opened and he sighed, seeing his parole officer and lawyer. It got to be some shit.

"Calm down Kareem, their just here for a check up." principle Grint said, but he still wasnt at ease. That parole officer put him through hell and the lawyer didnt even defend him. Yes his hands were registered because he had a temper but he had never sold drugs, but he was charged for it. "Can we keep dis short?" He asked, sitting on the leather couch and the principle nodded, closing the door.

"So." She started, going around her desk and sitting down. "Kareem is an amazing student." She said, with a smile and the parole officer chuckled. Kareem raised an eyebrow, mugging him. "Some funny?" He asked, and the officer nodded. "The fact that she think you're an amazing student. Aint no way some drug dealer can make a good stude- Say man ian finna listen to dis shit." Kareem cut him off, standing and pulling up his jeans. "Pitiful." The lawyer mumbled, and Kareem started to mug him as well.

"Listen hea, you two mutha fuckas bet not eva say shit ta me again. I been washed my hands witchall so stop coming around tryna fuck shit up cause in a minute imma fuck yall up. " He spoke as he pointed, feeling himself grow angrier. He hated the fact that his freedom was taken from him for even the few months he was in jail, of course he was let out because it was found that he wasnt the person they were looking for. It bothered him that just because of what he looks like, he wasn't able to see his family for months.

The lawyer smirked, amused by his anger. "You can say all that but once a thug always a thug." He said, and Kareem took a deep breath to keep from beating his ass. "Ms Grint imma see ya lata but yall." He looked to the officer and lawyer. "Yall can go ta hell." He nodded, turning around and leaving out the office. He so badly wanted to whoop their ass, because he knew he could but he also knew he shouldnt.

He had things to do, and a hopefully a good day ahead of him. He was not gonna let them ruin the day that barely start-ed. He grabbed the glass door, walking out the building and going towards the elective's area. He was gonna meet with the basketball coach, and try to get a spot on the team.

Coming up on the building he walked into the gym looking around the huge space. The bleachers are higher up, like a stadium and the court is humongous. "Can I help you?" Coach Brian asked, spotting Kareem from his office. Kareem turned to his left, nodding. "Yea im Kareem Jhonson n I was wondering if I could try out or some." He said, walking towards Brian.

Brian nodded, extending his hand and Kareem gave it a good shake. Which Brian noticed, a firm handshake is always good. "You played before?" Brian asked Kareem, allowing him into the office and Kareem nodded. "Back in high school."

He had heard about Kareem from Principle Grint, and from what she said and the clips he had seen of Kareem online of him playing basketball and running track in high school, he has a future for sure if he was to take that route. "Imma keep it real, principle Grint already got me convinced to just let you in hea but." He paused and Kareem nodded. "Ion do dat, everybody gotta try out so even though yours wont be official ill just have you come in on Friday to practice with the boys so I can see watchu working wit." He explained and Kareem smiled, continuing to nod.

He was excited, he always thought he'd play pro ball or run track professionally but after he graduated high school those few months in jail threw him off. With him being young it wasnt easy because the other men thought they could bitch him and make him do as they say, but that was indeed not the case. Kareem ended up getting put into solitary confinement for the rest of his sentence after he had gotten into a brawl with three other men. He wasnt a punk so he wasnt going to act like one.

Plus, he didnt know how to control his temper back then. That's the reason why his hands were registerd, once he found out his younger sister whom is only a year under him was getting beat by her boyfriend he lost his mind. That was his first strike. The next was when he came home one day to see his siblings with bruises and more, he almost killed his step father that day but he wouldnt dare touch his mother even though she allowed her husband to beat her kids to pay for her cheating. Thats the reason he moved him and his siblings into his grandmother's home, that was his second strike. Now, he's hanging on by a thread and he hoped that he could control his temper or he'd end up in jail, again.

"Well." Brian said, sighing. "Ill see you friday." He extended his hand again and kareem shook it, as he pulled him into a manly hug and they patted each other's back. "I appreciate it." Kareem said, pulling back from the hug and Brian nodded before Kareem left his office and walked out the building.

Brian hoped he wasnt making a mistake with this kid.

Pulling his phone out of his back pocket Kareem seen the that the time was only seven o' four. He definitely woke up too early, but he knew Dove was probably just getting up being that she has classes today.

He has a job interview to go to but he also has a little time to spare so why not get her some breakfast.

It took about eight minutes in total for him to get her a egg and ham english muffin with an iced coffee from Dunkin Donuts in the dining hall, before walking to her dorm.

He had knocked a few times and he went to knock again, just when she opened the door. "Hey! I didnt know you were coming by, I got classes." She said, stepping to the side so he could walk in and he nodded. "I know, but I brought you dis." He placed the brown bag on her desk, sipping from the coffee. "Thank's." She thanked him and he waved his hand. "I thought you said that was for me.." She said, making the duck lipped face as she pointed to the coffee he was drinking.

He nodded, observing her outfit. She wore a burgundy long sleeved shirt that stopped at her waist and to him it looked tight because the way it was showing of her breast. "It is for you but sharing is caring, and you putting on a jacket or some right?" He asked and she turned around walking to her closet. "Its cold outside?" She asked, thinking about what jacket could go with her outfit. She didnt really plan on wearing a jacket, maybe a sweater.

Kareem bit his bottom lip looking at her ass in the black leggings and the thigh high black heel boots didnt make it better, he thought it made her look sexier. "Put on a long jacket too." He said, and she turned around looking at him confused. "Why?"

"Or you could just change, yean going no where but to class." He added, the way she was looking was making him feel some kind of way and he didnt appreciate it.

She shook her head. "I got a lunch date after classes, and give me my drink." She said, reaching for the coffee and he furrowed his eyebrows moving to the side while sipping from the straw. He finally passed it to her and she rolled her eyes, seeing he downed half of it. "Date?" He asked, as she sipped from the straw and she nodded before putting the cup on her desk.

"Yea, and im actually excited. I met her last night in the dining hall and she is so funny and she's really pretty too." Dove said, and Kareem furrowed his eyebrows. "You gay? I mean aint none wrong wit dat if das make you happy but lemme know some." He said, and she looked at him like he had three heads. "What?" She asked, confused as to why he would think that. She has nothing against gay people but da cookie aint ha favorite treat.

"You said you gotta lunch dat- Nooo Kareem." She cut him off, laughing and he looked at her still confused. "Its not a date like dat, its just how you say lunch I guess." She sorta explained, shrugging and he nodded. "Bet not hadda been no date." He mumbled, pulling her into a hug and and she raised an eyebrow. "And why not?"

He pulled back from the hug, smirking. "Cause you off limits, have a good day doe." He said, going towards the door and she stood there smiling with her arms crossed over her chest.

"Dont forget ta put a jacket on eitha!" He yelled, closing the door.

She rolled her eyes and stood there for a good two minutes before going to her closet, looking for a sweater. She convinced herself it was because she wanted to and not because Kareem said so. After putting on a black and fashionable trench coat, she put on her gold necklace with her name engraved on a small bar and some small gold hoops.

She grabbed her purse then her phone seeing a notification pop up. After typing in her password she went to the messages app and ignored the one from her mom, pressing on Kareem's name.

Kareem: Betta had put a jacket on, ian playing

she rolled her eyes as she typed.

Dove: Boy go to hell

Kareem: Only if you come wimme

She chuckled, shaking her head. He really is a piece of work.

Kareem: Have a good day doe n pay attention in class!

She smiled as she typed.

Dove: Yes sir!  but good luck with your job interview, ian forget

Kareem smiled at his phone. If he was being honest he thought she had forgotten.

Kareem: Thank you ma

Dove clicked her phone off, stuffing it in the pocket of her trench coat before grabbing a hair tie off of her night stand and tying her hair up in a messy bun.

She looked at herself in the mirror before shaking her head. After taking the bun down she did it about three more times before saying fuck it, simply because she doesnt want to be late for class.

"Good enough..." She mumbled, looking at herself in the mirror. "Naw..." She said, taking her coat off and throwing it on her bed. She ended up changing her outfit three more times, something she'd end up doing everyday. She just didnt feel cute in anything and being that people didint really socialize with her, she thought the way she dressed or something about her was the reason so she always changed even if she did like what she was wearing.

Thats just her mental state at the moment...

# Chapter 6

------------------------------------------------------------

"I'm sorry momma but you were bringing my moo- I wasnt finished." Tasha chimed in, glaring at her daughter. Dove silenced herself, looking down at her white acrylic nails. "As I was saying. You have one more time to ignore me little girl and youll be coming home in less than an hour of me sending the text." Tasha said, looking around the small dorm. "And this dorm, I know I payed for better than this." She said, waving her hand around and Dove sighed. "Technically, I payed for it but ok." Nathan mumbled, sipping from his coffee and Tasha cut her eyes at him. "It's not the time Nathan."

He shrugged, leaning on Dove's desk. Tasha continued to lecture Dove as Nathan looked to the left of him, spotting Dove's phone which was silently ringing. He raised an eyebrow at the picture of Kareem and Dove sticking their tongue's out while crossing their eyes. "Who is this?" He asked, catching Dove and Tasha's attention. He held up her phone and Dove stood going to reach for it but Tasha grabbed her arm, taking the phone.

"Is this why you've been ignoring me?" Tasha asked, looking down at the picture of her daughter and some....boy.

"N- " Dove started to speak but was interrupted. "I should take your phone, you're letting a little boy keep you from contacting your family? He isnt even worth all that, by the looks of him.." Tasha mumbled, and Dove raised an eyebrow about to speak but turned her attention to the knocking on her door. Walking towards it, she prayed and hoped it wasnt him.

She unlocked the door and twisted the knob. "Jeese, no who is or anything.." Tasha mumbled, shaking her head. The door opened and Dove's heart beat quickened as he looked up at Kareem seeing his worried expression. "You good? Everything straight?" He asked, wondering why she was blocking him from entering her dorm. He wanted to go celebrate with her being that earlier he had gotten the call letting him know he received the job at a school for the saturday gym teacher. It wasnt much, but it was something. In Mentone schools tend to open school on saturday for those students who want to get ahead or excell.

Dove not answering his call was out of the ordinary, he wasnt gonna trip though because maybe she didn't want to be bothered. He just stopped by to check on her.

"Im fi- Who is that?" Tasha asked, walking towards Dove. Kareem raised an eyebrow at the unfamiliar voice, it wasnt Gia. "Move." Tasha said, pushing Dove out of her way and Dove scoffed staring at her mother. For some reason Tasha always felt the need to touch her, and it bothers Dove to the extreme.

Tasha frowned seeing Kareem, and Kareem sent her a small smile ignoring the look she was giving him. "I think you have the wrong dorm, have a nice da- He is at the right dorm." Dove said, stopping her mother from closing the door and Nathan raised his eyebrows at the sound of He.

"What do you mean he is at the right dorm?" Tasha asked, mugging Dove and Dove grabbed Kareem's hand pulling him into the room. Nathan almost spit out his coffee. "Who the hell is he!" He yelled, and Dove cleared her throat. "Momma, daddy. This is my friend Kareem." Dove introduced him, and Kareem extended his hand to Nathan but all Nathan did was mug him. Kareem was trying to be cool but he could feel the bad vibes coming from her parent's and he didnt like them, at all.

Plus, he was shocked himself when she called them momma and daddy being that they're white but his shock quickly went away because he doesn't know their situation so he wasnt about to judge so quickly, unlike them.

"Um, Hello.." Tasha greeted him, and Kareem sent her a head nod, letting his hand hang seeing that Nathan wasnt going to shake it. "Hey, nice to meet you." Kareem spoke to Tasha, not bothering to try and shake her hand. "Let his damn hand go." Nathan said, mugging Dove and she looked down noticing she was still holding his hand, she was actually holding on pretty tight at her nervous state and Kareem could tell something was making her uneasy.

"Natha- Dove let his damn hand go. You cant hea!" Nathan yelled, sitting his coffee down and Dove quickly removed her hand out of Kareem's grip, flinching a little. Kareem didnt like what he just seen, not one bit. The flinch is what bothered him the most, but the fact that her father was being so harsh about hand holding confused him. "When I tell you to do some girl, you best do it." Nathan pointed, and Dove looked into his eyes before quickly looking down at her white ankle socks.

"You here me?" Nathan asked and she nodded. He was putting her in a bad place, a horrible place and she was having a lot of flash backs. The belt was flying all over the place and all Dove felt was pain, Nathan was putting all his might into the hits and he wasnt gonna stop anytime soon. "Im sorry!" She yelled, only infuriating him more. Tasha nodded, as she watched her husband what they called beat the black off their eight year old adopted daughter. Tasha was about to do her hair but Dove wasnt cooperating, she was tired of getting perms and relaxer's. She wanted to leave her hair how it was but Tasha didnt like how her hair was, she felt like it made her look nasty and even more ugly. That was the last day Dove ever put up a fight against anything her parents wanted, she was gonna do anything to please them, anything to not get beat again. But best believe, when she came of age she did the big chop right away then let her hair grow before starting her loc's.

"Dove you good?" Kareem asked, touching her shoulder and Nathan mugged him. "You betta take yo hands off my daughter." He forcefully spoke, causing Kareem to raise an eyebrow but he calmed his self down. "Im fine Kareem.." Dove mumbled, removing his hand from her shoulder earning a smile from Tasha but a shocked look from Kareem. "You should go, or do I need to escort you out?" Nathan asked, continuing to mug the thug standing in front of him. He could tell just by how his jeans were sagging, and the color of his skin said it all.

Kareem looked to Nathan now with a mug of his own. "Was yo proble- My problem is you harassing my daughter, calling her phone then showing up here. Do I need to report you?" Nathan asked and Kareem looked down at Dove. "So das what im doing? Im harassing you?" He asked, feeling like thats what she told them. Dove started to deny it but by the way her father was looking at her she felt she'd regret saying anything so she didnt speak. "Dove." Tasha urged her and Dove cleared her throat. "Y- yea..." She mumbled, voice shaky as her vision started to blur with the forming tears.

Kareem continued to look down at her as she looked down at her socks, wiping her tears. He scoffed, slowly nodding. "Aight den." He said, before going towards the door and Nathan followed going to grab his arm but Kareem pushed his hand. "Dont touch me dawg, ian playing." He warned, finally reaching the door and Nathan grabbed his arm causing him to turn around and punch him in his left jaw. "Nathan!" Tasha yelled, rushing to his aid down on the floor and Dove's eyes grew big and Kareem exited her dorm, slamming the door.

He'd be lying if he said her words just then didnt hurt but he wasn't going to dwell on it. If that's how she wanted to be then so be it. All he was worried about was her family pressing charges, because he knew he broke her father's jaw.

# Chapter 7

Gia sighed, looking at a pained Dove. "You sure you dont want to go out? Or like, just walk around campus?" Gia asked, standing from the rolling chair and Dove shook her head, typing her tenth message today to Kareem. She knew she was blocked but she didnt care. "You still tryna text him?" Gia asked, noticing Dove's thumbs moving quit fast on the screen.

Dove sighed, clicking her phone off and throwing it beside her. "I messed up. I get it, but at least he could let me explain." Dove said, crossing her arms. She knew what she said was wrong but it was like she wasnt even in control of herself, like she could see what was happening but she wasnt actually present.

Dove had explained to Gia everything that happened, and Gia was overwhelmed just from hearing the story. The whole situation was a mess, and when Dove spoke about her parents

Gia was enraged. She couldnt see how people could be so heartless, and cruel. Especially to a child.

"If you dont mind me asking." Gia started, and Dove raised an eyebrow looking to her friend just of a couple of weeks. "You've known him longer than you know me but you told me some deep shit. How come you cant just tell him?" Gia asked, truly curious. Dove had let all her feelings and emotions go when speaking to Gia but for some reason she couldnt see herself doing that with Kareem. Why? She didnt know but it was something telling her that he would look at her differently.

"I kind of dont want to talk about it anymore.." Dove said, hoping Gia would understand and she did. "That's cool, but I have one more question." Gia said, holding up her index finger which showcased her bright yellow acrylic nails with rhine-stones. The yellow really complemented her beautiful dark chocolate skin. "How bad you wanna see him?" Gia asked, with her lips curving into a smirk. "What you mean?" Dove asked, raising both her eyebrows at the look Gia was sending her. "Dont worry bout it, but ay." She called, pulling on her gray puffer coat. "Put on some..cute. Y'know, besides the sweats n shirt." Gia said, looking over Dove's attire. You could tell she's in her feelings, looking like she dont love herself.

"So im not cut- Girl shut up and put on some sexy!" Gia yelled, waving her hand around and Dove couldnt help but smile, while rolling her eyes. "Mhm. Now I would say ill be back but thats a lie." Gia shrugged, before going towards the door and Dove chuckled while going towards her closet.

Even though Gia didnt know Dove like that, if she felt comfortable enough to tell her all that she did then she could help her out a little. Plus, Gia doesnt mind making new friends. Being that she didnt have many but the ones back home.

She pushed her braids over her shoulder while walking towards the elective's building. "Ay!" She yelled, and the white boy walking out the building raised his eyebrows. He started to look around and she rolled her eyes, approaching him. "Boy toughen up, aint nobody finna hurt you." She said, seeing his nervous expression and weird stance.

Thats one of the things she hated, being racially profiled and judged by others. She's been judged a lot just by her liking women so with her being black, it doesnt make things easier. "Is da basketball team still in dere?" She asked, pointing towards the glass door and the boy nodded, hoping this conversation could be over fast.

Gia sent him a big smile, slapping his shoulder causing him to flinch. "Thanks pal!" She yelled, walking into the building and he scurried away.

Whistles filled the gym, causing Kareem to turn around and he shook his head seeing Gia stand there glaring at him. "For one, yall can settle the fuck down cause imma cat girl. Anyway! Kareem may I have a word with you?" Gia asked, walking towards him with a smirk, being that all the guys had went quiet hearing she was gay. "Whatchu want Gia?" Kareem asked, not really in the mood.

He was tired, hungry and sleepy. Plus, even though he asked. He already know's what she wants and he doesnt want to hear it. He would have been started back talking to Dove a few weeks ago but when he found out her parents were trying to press charges, it just pushed him farther away from her. Luckily Principle Grint talked the Dasani's out of it but Kareem was close to being sentenced again, and that was them messing with his education, which messed with his future, which messed with his money and families well being. He wasnt for allat.

"Why you ignoring my home girl? Got ha looking like a lost puppy n shit." Gia said, following Kareem out the gym and he shrugged opening the glass door, allowing her to walk out the building then he followed. "Is that all you tryna talk bout?" He asked, going towards the dining hall. Some McDonalds sound real good to him at the moment.

Gia scrunched her face up, stopping in her tracks. Never did he just talk about Dove like she wasnt nothing, well technically he didnt. He was speaking about the situation but thats not how Gia seen it. "First of all, you needa stop acting like a little bitch about one lil sentence and man up and listen to ha!" Gia yelled, causing him to turn around with a raised eyebrow. Her stance faltered a little but thats only because he's so damn big!

Kareem chuckled, that whole little outburst she just had was hilarious to him. A bitch? Please. Never had he ever been one and never will he be. "Fo one, ian tryna be on no usher shit but nigga's got emotions too. N I would be lying if I said what she said aint hurt me cause it did. She a coo lil lady n fo ha to say some weird shit like dat bothered me. N it still do. So, im finna go get me a burger n gone bout my night. Bye." Kareem said, sending her a head nod before walking towards the dining hall.

Gia stood there with her arms crossed, squinting her eyes at him. She was one to get what she wants, when she wants it. So for him to just brush off everything she said, it bothered her. "Kareem!" She yelled, following him. She was determined for Dove to be happy, or at least to explain.

Gia could tell Dove's a nice person, too nice some would say and she made one mistake. Kareem has to forgive her!

"What Gia damn!" Kareem yelled, turning around. Now with a mug on his face and Gia sighed. "Just give her a chance to explain! Pleaseeee!" Gia begged, batting her eye lashes and Kareem scrunched up his face. "Stop doing dat, you look ugly." He joked and she smacked her lips, trying not to laugh. "If youn go talk to ha, imma tell yo coach you been eating McDonalds n he gone make you do extra drills." She said, with a smirk and Kareem cut his eyes at her.

"How you kno- Just cause im gay dont mean I cant get a lil head from a pillow talking basketball player, now go n talk to my friend! After you take a shower. Cause yo ass smell like dead racoons n ten cans out bounce dat ass. Now bye." Gia mushed his head, before turning around and walking towards her dorm.

Kareem pulled the plain blue shirt over his head, sighing. He wasnt gonna bother with any chains or none of that, being that he didnt see reason for it. After slipping into his nike slides he turned his speaker off and connected his phone to his charger, before grabbing his keys and walking out of his dorm. He would lie and say that Gia's blackmail was the only reason he was going to see Dove but it wasnt. He does indeed miss her.

As soon as he stepped outside he became cold, because of the weather and his dripping curls. His hair was always curly after a shower.

It didnt take him long to reach Dove's building, being that he was rushing to get there because it was too cold outside. Arriving in front of her door, he was about to turn around but he felt like that was a bitch move so he knocked.

Dove checked her phone to see if Gia had texted her back yet but she hadnt even read one message. Why would she tell her to dress up then not communicate? It didnt make sense to Dove and it annoyed her, being that she could've still been in sweats right now.

Another knock was heard on her door and she stood going towards it, with the sound of her beige heel's clanking on the wooden floor. She opened the door thinking it would be Gia, but the face she seen caused her to blink a couple times.

Kareem jerked his head back, looking her over. For one, the baby blue dress was too short, it didnt even reach her knee's and it not having straps left her shoulders and some of her chest exposed. The little silver necklace only brought more attention to it. He hair was down too, when did she start doing that? All that was going through his head is who she wearing her hair down for?

"Ion know wea da fuck you thought you was going but yean going." He said, focusing on her thighs and she clenched her legs together, which he noticed and he wanted to smirk but it wasnt the time for that.

He finally looked up, into her eyes and she stood there frozen. It was like everything she wanted to say to him was out of her mind. She was stuck. "Im sorry. I didnt mean it, I was just in a bad place all of a sudden and the- "

Her eyes grew big, at the feeling of his soft lips on her's. She was once again, stuck.

He bit her bottom lip for access, and his tounge did the rest.

His hands went from her waist to her ass once she finally started to kiss him back, closing her eyes.

Pulling back from the kiss, they looked into each other's eyes for a good two minutes before laughing. "So, you forgive me?" Dove asked, and he lifted her legs until she was straddling him causing her to wrap her arms around his neck, at the abrupt motion. "Yea I forgive you Dove." He truthfully spoke, looking into her eyes and she her smile grew.

He started to walk them into her dorm and her heart beat quickened. "Calm down lil love, we aint finna do nun but watch a movie. Afta you change, or some really gone happen." Kareem said, closing the door and locking it with his right hand while holding her with his left.

Dove relaxed, laying her head on his chest. "I missed you.." She admitted and he smiled. "I miss you too." He replied, sitting on her bed.

"Watchu wanna watch?" He asked, grabbing the remote.

"Friday!" Dove yelled, talking about her new favorite movie, which Kareem put her on too. He chuckled typing it in on the television.

"Bet.." He said, before putting the remote beside them and looking into her eyes again. "Dont eva do no shit like dat again. Got me?" He asked n she nodded.

"Gotchu.."

# Chapter 8

"No Dove, now move." Kareem said, mushing her head and she smacked her lips, sitting beside him on his bed. "Just try a little bit." She begged, holding out the platic spoon with mint chocolate chip ice cream out to him and he shook his head. "Dat shit look weird, just like you is fo eating."

"Youn neva wanna try nun new!" Dove yelled, sticking the spoon in her mouth and Kareem smirked at the way she just spoke. "Youn neva wann- Shut up!" Dove yelled, mushing his head and they started laughing before turning their attention back to the television which played, Tyler Perry - Diary of a mad black woman.

"and im not bitter, Im mad as hell!": The woman on the screen yelled, before walking off and Dove nodded.

"Period ms gurl!!" Dove yelled, pursing her lips together as she watched the movie. Kareem smiled, while eating some of his Ice cream, regular ol' cookies and cream. Whenever they would watch a movie, she would be so into it. She was starting to remind him of his sisters, and he knew they'd get along well just by seeing how Dove and Gia act with each other even though they have two different personalities.

"Kareem." Dove called, staring at the television and he looked over to her with a raised eyebrow. "Hmm?" He hummed and she tried not to smile. "Gimme kiss." She said, leaning towards him and he smirked pecking her lips, causing her to slap his arm. "A real kiss stupid!"

He smiled, grabbing her face and pecking her lips again before sliding his tongue in her mouth and deepening the kiss, causing her to smile against his lips. She thought she was slick but he already knew what she was trying to do. They pulled back from the kiss, and she happily grabbed her ice cream thinking her plan was successful.

"N yean slick eitha, You just wanted me to taste dat nasty ass ice cream." Kareem said, staring at the television as he ate a spoon of cookies and cream and Dove's mouth fell open causing him to laugh. "Oh my gosh! Cant never get away with shit!" She yelled, sitting her ice cream down. She didnt even want it no more, anything she tried to do it was like he was a step ahead of her. Kareem only laughed harder at her little attitude she just grew. He stood up, continuing to chuckle as he placed his ice cream beside her's on the night stand.

Observing her face he couldnt help but laugh, her bottom lip was all poked out and her arms were crossed over her chest. "Dove." He called, placing himself in-between her legs. "Move

Kareem." She said, pushing his stomach back and he chuckled seeing her cheeks turn red. "Lemme find out." He joked, rubbing her thighs and she slapped his hands. "Just annoying, Move!" She yelled, trying not to smile. He wouldn't even allow her to be mad at him, he was always tryna play and she'd end up giving in.

He grabbed her arms, placing them above her head while smirking at her and she bust out laughing. "Yeaaa das wat I like ta see." Kareem said, smiling because she was smiling. "Boy fuck you!" Dove yelled, trying to get her hands out of his grip. "I mean..." Kareem mumbled, raising his eyebrows and her smile dropped. "Stop playing." She told him, feeling butterflies in her stomach.

"Scary ass." He smirked, letting her hands go and she rolled her eyes grabbing her ice cream. He was always making lil slick jokes and she'd end up being stuck, like always. She didnt know what to do or say.

"Wat dat girl said?" Kareem asked causing Dove to raise an eyebrow. "All dese girls wanna fuck Kareem! Dey do!" He yelled, rolling his neck and Dove bust out laughing. "Hellcat some, some, some." He continued to yell, not knowing the rest of the lyrics and Dove clutched her stomach continuing to laugh.

"Kareem stop you making my stomach hurt!" She yelled, trying to stop laughing and he smirked. "Dat aint da only way ill make yo stomach hur- "

He was interrupted by his ringing phone, and Dove was thankful because she knew what he was getting at.

"Reem!" Keyonna yelled, as soon as the call connected and Kareem smiled, sitting down in Dove's rolling chair. "Wassup Kee!" He greeted her, and she smiled showing her lil sna-ga toothed smile. "Watchu doing?" Keyonna asked, plopping down on her grandmother's soft couch. "Im wit my friend, wanna say hi?" Kareem asked, looking up at a big eyed Dove. Now why is he playing.

"Its a girl! Yea!" Keyonna yelled, excited. The only girl friend she knew Kareem had was Malina. Kareem stood up and Dove mugged him, while shaking her head. She wasnt ready to meet-well talk to any of his family just yet. "Kareem sto- Hi!" Dove waved, and Keyonna smiled again. "Hi! You so pretty!" Keyon-na complimented her and Dove smiled.

"You're pretty too!" Dove said, and Keyonna furrowed her eyebrows. "Reem why ha sound like dat? Was a Yur?" Keyonna asked, causing Dove and Kareem to laugh. "Its you're Kee." Ka-reem corrected her and she nodded. "Yur?" She repeated but they laughed again. "You're." Dove said, slowly pronouncing it. "Oh ok, Youre?" Keyonna asked, and they nodded causing her to smile.

"Somebody take dis damn baby!" T'suniya yelled, stepping into her grandmother's house, holding Lauren's son.

Kareem chuckled, at the voice of his cousin. "Niya Reem on da phone!" Keyonna yelled, as Lauren took Aubrey from

T'suniya. "Ooo, my favorite cousin! Wea he at? Ian seen him in a minute." T'suniya said, sitting down next to Keyonna and Lauren smacked her lips. "Bitch, he in college da fuck. How you forget?"

T'suniya held her hand up. "Not too much on me ms mam." She put up the middle finger before looking at the phone, hearing Kareem laughing. "Hey favorite cousin!" She yelled, and Keyonna mugged her. "You in my ear Niya..." Keyonna mumbled, and T'suniya mugged her.

"Im finna stop coming ova hea cause oooweee." She said, standing up as her grandmother walked down the hall. "What's all this yelling going on in my house? Yall asses just need to g- Kareem on da phone." Lauren said, not wanting to hear her grandmother go on and on.

"My grandbaby?" Carol asked, growing a smile and Lauren rolled her eyes. "Who else granny?"

"Ay chillat talking ta granny like dat!" Kareem yelled, to his younger sister and Lauren came into the camera just to throw up the middle finger, causing Dove to silently chuckle.

This was new to her, the way they interacted. She...like's it.

"Ooo, who is she?" T'suniya asked, observing the pretty girl beside her cousin. "Notcho ugly ass." Marco said, mushing her head and looking at da screen. "Wassup brody! How ya feel?" Marco asked his big brother, and Kareem shrugged. "Im striaght but damn can I see granny, all you bastards in da phone!" He yelled, causing all of them to laugh. Including Lauren.

Carol pushed her grandchildren out the way, so she could receive the phone. "Hey baby!" She said, smiling at her favorite grandchild. It was true, and she they all know. She has no shame in it either. He's more responsible than the rest and more respectful, even little Keyonna had a bad attitude sometimes.

"Wassup Granny!" Kareem greeted her, with a big smile. Dove had been watching his expression the whole time, and he hadnt stopped smiling yet. She could tell he misses them. "Who is dat?" Carol asked, squinting her eyes at Dove and Dove stopped staring at Kareem to look at the phone, with a small smile. "Dis is Dove." Kareem virtually introduced her and Carol smirked. "Mm." She hummed. "Hi." Dove said, waving. Nervous was a understatement, and they weren't even in person. "Hey baby, nice to meet you." Carol said, looking at the pretty girl. She just wondered if she was smart.

"Nice to meet you too Ms Jhons- Granny girl. Yean gotta be all professionol wit ha old ass!" T'suniya yelled, from the kitchen as she looked in the oven seeing her granny making macaroni to go with the fried chicken and greens.

Dove chuckled, as Carol mugged T'suniya. "Im finna start whooping ass!" She yelled, placing the phone on the table and Kareem shook his head laughing. "Das my que ta go." T'suniya said, taking her plate and going towards the door.

Thats one thing about their grandmother, she didnt care how old they got. Everybody could be her belts best friend.

Lauren sighed, picking up the phone. She had some stuff to clear up with her older brother. Dove noticed Kareem's expression change, as he stood up. "You ok?" She asked, watching him go towards the door. "Yea ill be back, order some food or some." Kareem responded, before stepping out of her dorm.

Lauren stood up and walked back into her room, in her grandmother's house. "Imma say dis one time Lauren. If I find out you still fucking wit dat nigg- Aint nobody messing wit him no mo Kareem. You needa let dat go!" Lauren yelled, mugging him through the screen. "Shut the fuck up and listen!" Kareem yelled, and Dove raised her eyebrow's hearing him from in the room.

She was gonna mind her business and continue ordering this food.

Lauren rolled her eye's, but shut up. "Not only did you fuck wit dis nigga when I told you not too! You ended up having his baby, while he was beating yo ass!" Kareem stated, and Lauren looked down. She was annoyed at the fact he was always throwing it in her face. Like, ok she got it. She fucked up but he wouldnt let the shit go.

The only reason Kareem wont let it go is because he has a gut feeling that she hasnt let the nigga go. "Now, if I find out you still fucking wit him. Imma come home n we gone have some serious issues. Im not playing witchu Lauren n das on granny."

Kareem calmly stated, and Lauren felt a jolt of nervousness run through her body. "Love you." He said, trying to shake this feeling he was getting. Something was telling him to go home and just forget about school.

"Love you too." Lauren quickly said, before hanging up the phone. She looked down at Aubrey, whom was sleep in her arms. "Yo daddy gone get us in trouble.." She whispered, before standing up to pack their bags, to go to Anthony's for the weekend.

# Chapter 9

----------------------------------------------------------------

"**N**ow what am I supposed to do, when I want you in my world!"

Kareem, rolled over with a mug on his face. He reached on Dove's night stand and grabbed his phone, clicking it on. Seeing the time was after twelve he sat up with a sigh.

"How can I want you for myself, When Im already someone's Girllll" Dove continued to sing Erykah Badu - Next lifetime, as she washed her body. She'd usually wait until Kareem fell asleep to take a shower, being that she always sings.

"Oh shit.." Kareem mumbled, listening to Dove sing. He was astonished but she sound's good as hell. Part of him was wondering why he didnt know of this talent yet but he was too busy listening to dwell on it.

Dove continued to sing, stepping out of the shower and wrapping a light pink towel around her. After drying off and applying some baby lotion so took her loc's out the bun they were in and threw the hair tie on the sinks counter. She need's to re-twist her hair but that can wait until tomorrow.

As she sung along with Erykah she walked out the bathroom doing a little dance, causing Kareem to silently chuckle. Its like she's a whole different person when she's by herself, or thinks nobody is watching.

"I guess ill see you next lifetim- " She stopped her sentence, feeling his hands go around her waist. She couldnt believe it. How long has he been up?

"Kare- So you can sing." He said, turning her around and she sighed covering her face. Which caused him to mug her. "Fuck you embarrassed fo?" He asked, confused. From what he heard she need to be trying to let the whole world hear her voice. "Why was you ease dropping on me?" She asked, trying to turn the situation on him, and he chuckled. "I asked you a question first, n yo ass was loud as hell. Woke a nigga up. But you sound good so ion mind." He shrugged and Dove shook her head. She felt like he was lying.

"Did I for real?" She asked, and he leaned his head back. "Man do you hea yo self?" He asked, backing up from her and Dove raised her eyebrows. "You was like, What am I supposed ta do n den I was like Ohhhhh shit!" He yelled, covering his mouth and she chuckled.

"Got me thinking im at a concert or some shit, but den listen. Dis my favorite part. When you was like, I guess ill se you next

LifeTiMeeEee!" He repeated what she sang, and she continued to laugh. She just knew she was blushing.

Kareem nodded. He was serious, her voice is some different. "Sounding like Beyoncé n shit." He said, trying to act all nonchalant about it and Dove's cheeks were starting to hurt she was smiling so much. "Dont gas me.." She mumbled, shaking her head and he smacked his lips. "For real doe. You got some ta work wit cause ian even know dat was you." He complimented her and she started smiling again. "Thank you Kareem Damn! Yean gotta keep going!" She yelled, chuckling a little.

"Im gone keep going, cause you- " He stopped his sentence, lifting her in the air and her eyes grew big as he spun them around. "Deserve it!" He yelled, laying her on the bed.

She smiled at him as he rubbed her thighs. "Sing my name." He told her, biting his bottom lip. "Boy if you dont gone." She said, mushing his head and he smiled. "Come on Dove, sing it." He said, pecking her lips and she shook her head, trying not to smile.

Bet. He started to deepen the kiss as he pulled her to he edge of the bed and her arms wrapped around his neck. "Im still not boutta s- Kareem stop playing." Dove said, feeling his lips on her neck, causing her to bite her bottom lip.

"Hmm?" He hummed, squeezing her thighs as he started to suck on the spot he noticed caused her to be quiet. Dove's eyes were shut tight as she felt his hand slip under the long shirt she was wearing. "Kareem!" She yelled, as he did a lil finger work.

He removed his hand, as he stood up straight, with a huge grin on his face.

"Im satisfied but you not." He teased, licking his fingers and Dove glared at him. "Get the fuck out!" She yelled, pointing to the door and he bust out laughing.

"Just stupid." She continued to pout, sitting up and crossing her arms. As Kareem continued to laugh. All she had to do was sing his name, but she wanted to go the hard way.

"Im finna go, I got work in da morning. Gimme a kiss." He said, leaning in and he was met with a pillow. "Kiss my ass!" Dove yelled, hitting him with the pillow again and he started back laughing. "Glad to." Kareem replied, before walking towards the door.

"Wait!" Dove yelled, standing up and he turned around with a smirk. "Be safe, n bring me some breakfast in the morning." She said, kissing his cheek and he smiled, opening the door. "I gotchu."

He stepped out of the dorm and she went to follow him, since she usually watches him down the hall. "Take yo ass back in dat room." He said, mugging her and she looked at him with a mug of her own.

"You mustve forgot you aint dressed properly but fa my eyes." He said, pushing her back into the room and she rolled her eyes. "You get on my nerves! Bye." She said, slamming the door and he crossed his arms, standing there.

Three minutes later, she opened the door. "Stupid." She mumbled, giving him a hug and he smiled knowing she was smiling too, and she was.

"Just annoying." Dove said, pulling back from the hug and he mushed her head before walking off towards the glass door, which was the exit.

Once he left the building Dove smiled going back into her dorm and closing the door. Wait till she tell Gia about this shit....

# Chapter 10

Anthony pulled up in front of Carol's house, peeking at Lauren from the corner of his eye. Once his black range rover was in park, he turned his head towards her, seeing her wipe a couple tears. "Whatchu crying for?" He asked, truly confused.

Lauren looked up at him with a mug on her beautiful face. "What the hell you me- Lower yo tone." Anthony calmly spoke, continuing to stare at her with cold eyes. Lauren shut her mouth, looking to her right out the window. "I said lower yo tone, not stop talking." Anthony spoke, while opening the glove compartment and grabbing a pack of backwoods.

Lauren ignored him, while shaking her head. What did he mean why was she crying? He just beat the hell out of her. Anthony chuckled grabbing his lighter from the cup holder. Her little attitude was cute to him. As he lit the wood Lauren turned to him with a scrunched up face. "You not finna smoke dat wit

Aubrey in the car." She told him, reaching for it but he pushed her back against the door. "Chill out. Fo I make yo ass chill out."

She pushed his arm and his hand flew right across her cheek, causing her to hold it with a horrified look. As she went to get out the car, he grabbed her arm. "Let me go!" She yelled, trying to get of his grip which only tightened. He sighed, throwing the wood out the window before grabbing Laurens body and holding her in the seat. "You must want me ta beatcho ass!" He yelled, and she continued to try and escape his grip. "It aint like you neva did befo- Ay!" T'suniya yelled, standing by Anthony's window with a mug on her face. Who the hell car parked outside of her granny's house.

Anthony was thankful for his tented window's, he knew he could beat Laurens ass and have her come back but if her brothers ever got involved he knew it would be a different story. "Now watchu gone do lil bitch?" Lauren asked, glaring at him and Anthony chuckled before his hand flew across her face again, but it didnt feel like a slap. Because it wasnt. He punched the hell out of her, causing her lip to bleed. "Keep on talking reckless imma show yo ass who da bitch." He roughly said, before letting her go and unlocking his doors.

T'suniya opened the door after hearing the click, she didnt care if it wasnt her car or not. They shouldnt be in her usual parking spot. Got her parking in the driveway, knowing her paw paw gone ask her to back out, and that take too much energy.

"Imma need you ta mo- Oh hell naw! I know you fucking lying!" T'suniya yelled, cutting her own sentence off once she seen Anthony. He smiled stepping out the car, T'suniya's a fine lil sum and he wouldt mind fucking wit her. Once he was done with Lauren. It's some bout them Jhonson girls.

Lauren rushed and grabbed Aubrey out the car, along with her belongings. "Lauren Lin!" T'suniya yelled, now ignoring Anthony's presence. Lauren ignored her cousin, trying to rush into the house. She needed to take care of her lip. T'suniya caught her at the door and once she seen her face, she instantly went to call Marco. "Marc- Niya shut up!" Lauren whisper yelled, covering T'suniya's mouth.

She was only trying to help her stupid ass. There was no way this girl should continue going back to this man whose treating her like shit. T'suniya slapped her hand away. "Bitch dont touch me, ion know wea da hell yo hands been n watchu mean be queit? If im remembering correctly aint dat da nigga dat Reem gotta strike fo, cause he beat his ass fo beating yo ass. Yea." T'suniya finished, nodding her head. She didnt know who the hell Lauren thought she was, but she dont have to listen to her.

"Marco!" T'suniya yelled again, stepping into her granny's house catching everybody's attention. Ooo, her paw paw's home. "Paw paw, dat boy dat was beating on Lauren outside!" T'suniya yelled, and Henderick got up from his seat, along with

Marco. "Da fuck is he hea fo." Marco mumbled, quickly walking past T'suniya.

"Oh lord.." Carol mumbled, standing from her seat and going to the sink. She reached in the cabinet under it and grabbed her husbands gun. "Granny whats that!" Keyonna yelled, chewing on some bacon. "Stay in yo place and eat dat food." Carol told her, before walking past T'suniya and heading outside.

One thing about them was, when it came to family. One goes down, they all go down. Thats why when Carol and Henderick found out about their daughter was letting her man beat her kids they almost went to jail's themselves. But, Kareem had already beat the man to near death and their daughter just wouldnt let them hurt him again. Carol made sure her grand-kid's knew they could come live with her and that they did. Even though they're a pain in her ass she loves them.

"Niya whats going o- " Glass breaking interrupted Keyonna's sentence causing her to flinch in her seat. "Come on lets go draw or some.." T'suniya said, trying to get Keyonna away from the front of the house which was farther away from the commotion. Keyonna nodded, before rushing to follow T'suniya down the hall. Little Keyonna was indeed scared, loud noises or any sudden moves scare her sometimes. She herself has been through a lot, at only eight years old.

# Chapter 11

"How many mo laps we got Mr K?" Simone asked, with her hands on her knee's as she tried to control her breathing. "Its the you being outta shap fo me." Malia said, jogging past her.

William chuckled along with the twins, Quincy and Quan. "Yall only got one mo Simone, n ion see nun funny cause yall lil nigga's aint ran not one lap." Kareem said, walking up to the three boys who were standing in the corner.

"Mr K it wasnt even me, dey was da ones tryna look at Malia while she run." Quincy snitched, holding his hands up in surrender and Kareem shook his head chuckling. They reminded him of Marco. "Yall wild, but come on. Yall class finna be over." He motioned for the boys to follow him, to the center of the court where the rest of the students were.

"Mr K my stomach hurt, can I got to da nurse?" Camari asked, with a frown and Kareem nodded. "Take da pass." He said, pointing to the pass on his desk and she nodded before head-ing that way.

Once they made it to the middle, the boys stood in line wait-ing for Kareem to speak like everyone else. "As far as partici-pation go, most of yall good." Kareem said, before eyeing the boys. "You lil nigga's, imma be on yall ass." He pointed and the class chuckled. "Not Mr K cussing." Maria said, pursing her lips together and everyone continued to laugh, including Kareem.

He enjoys his job, and the kids like him too. He's actually their favorite teacher. "We still having our pizza party?" Quan asked, catching everybody's attention. They forgot all about that. Ka-reem had his two classes of fifteen students play against each other in a basketball game, just for fun and to switch up the way he taught.

This class won in the end and he promised them a pizza par-ty. "Yea we gone have it tomor- Pizza dont sound so healthy." Dove said, walking through the gym doors and Kareem smiled as she walked towards them.

"Hey Mrs Dove!" Maria and Samone said at the same time, causing them to chuckle and Dove smiled, waving. "Misses D in da building!" Elijah yelled, and Dove continued to smile. The students liked her as well, they know her pretty well since she sat in on a few on their classes.

"She said she'll see what she can do, dey tryna call my mom-ma." Camari said, entering the gym again and Kareem nodded.

Dove came up beside Kareem and he raised an eyebrow. "Wea you going afta you leave hea?" He asked, observing her lil outfit she had on. Her hair was down, she was starting to wear it like that often and her dark brown skirt went with the cream colored sweater she wore to match her knee high boots. "Me, Gia going for lunch so I wanted ta bring you some." Dove responded, holding out the subway bag. "Neva did you get me some subway." Kareem said, looking down at the bag with a smirk. "I wasnt finna buy you no McDonalds. Yo coach said only healthy foods for at least a week." Dove said, with a smirk of her own.

"Dis nigga gotta eat subway." William joked, laughing with the twins and Kareem bust out laughing. "Get yall lil bad asses outta hea, da bell finna ring." He said, just before the bell rang and the students said their goodbye's before leaving the gym.

"For real doe, I appreciate it." Kareem said, giving her a quick kiss. "Finally I got away wit some!" Dove yelled, doing a little dance and Kareem looked at her confused. "Watchu mean?" He asked, and she pointed to the bag. "Its some taco bell in dere." She laughed, and he smacked his lips before laughing too. "You really went to subway just fo a bag ta prete- man." He waved his hand, just thinking about all she did to trick him.

"Its not my fault you be figuring out everything I do, so I wanted to try again." She grinned, and he shook his head walking towards his desk and she followed.

"Ion think I like yo outfit." Kareem said, causing her to furrow her eyebrows. "Why?" She asked, looking down at herself and he leaned against his desk pulling her closer to him, resting his hands on her waist. "Looking too good fo da public eye." He complimented her, with a smirk and she rolled her eyes. "Boy...shut up." She mumbled, looking away and he touched her chin, giving her a sweet kiss.

"Wea da lil gir- Unt unt! Not on duty! Not on duty!" Zaria yelled, seeing Kareem and Dove swallowing each others faces. Dove pulled back from the kiss, holding Kareem's shoulders as she laughed. He started laughing too, because he knew what she was thinking about. Dae Dae from Friday after next.

Kareem stood up straight, causing Dove to back up and let him go. "Watchu need Zaria?" He asked and she held up a ziploc bag of ice. "Dem mutha fuckas den told me ta bring dis girl some ice cause ha stomach hurt. N now she not even in hea no mo, see im boutta quit!" Zaria yelled, before exiting the gym and Kareem and Dove laughed.

"Im finna g- " Dove was interrupted by Kareem's ringing phone and he pulled it out his jogging pants pocket. "Whatchu was saying?" He asked, before accepting the call. "Im about to go, see you later." She whispered, and he leaned in for a quick kiss but she backed up, silently laughing at his expression.

He grabbed her arm, pulling her to him and pecking her lips before mushing her head. "Duck face ass." He whispered, trying not to let his granny hear him from the phone. "Lil dick ass." Dove shot back, and he raised an eyebrow. "How much you wanna be- Kareem is you listening to me?" Carol asked, catching Kareem's attention.

"Yea." He replied, and Dove smirked before heading to the gym doors.

# Chapter 12

"Ok granny I heard you!" Lauren yelled, gathering her and Aubrey's items. She was tired of hearing her grandmother go on and on about something that happened a week ago. Carol raised an eyebrow, standing in the door frame. "Who you raising your voice at?" She asked, standing up straight and Lauren rolled her eyes, stuffing some of Aubrey's clothes in a duffle bag.

"Lauren Lin Jhonson, answer me when im talk- What granny damn!" Lauren yelled, turning around with a mug on her face. "I know you not in hea talking ta granny like dat!" T'suniya yelled, walking down the hallway and Lauren rolled her eyes. "Why is you even hea? All ways ova hea." Lauren mumbled, zipping up the duffle bag.

"Girl just cause yo disrespectful ass live wit granny and see ha everyday dont mean I do." T'suniya said, walking past her granny into the room. Lauren shook her head, while putting on a jacket. "Where you bout to go?" Carol asked, crossing her arms. Lauren was so lost, and everybody could see it but her. She's a book smart beautiful eighteen year old but when it comes to knowing how life works and not to believe everything, she's dumb. Meaning, she's gullible.

"Im finna go to my nigga hou- The one who be beating yo ass?" T'suniya asked, scrunching her face up. "Dis shit is beyond muther fucking me." She shook her head, sitting on the queen sized bed.

"Niya." Carol said, in a warning tone and T'suniya held her hands up in surrender. "I wont say none else to ha stupid ass." T'suniya told her granny, while looking at her light blue coffin nails with glitter.

Lauren wanted to fight T'suniya so bad. She felt like she stuck her nose in places it didnt belong an that alone was good enough reason for a ass whoopin, but the cousins have fought before. Plenty of times, and they stayed arguing when they were little. There was never a determined winner because the fights would always get broke up, and each of the girls could hold their own.

T'suniya wasnt the cause of their bad relationship, it was all Lauren. Lauren didnt like how close T'suniya and Kareem were. Being that T'suniya was born in the same year as Kareem they were closer but when Lauren came along she felt like all his attention should have went to her, but the little bit that she felt she got was soon taken away by Marco, then Keyonna.

T'suniya felt like Lauren was one of those females who thought the world should revolve around her, and if something didnt go her way then everybody had to suffer. T'suniya also felt that Lauren was too stupid to think everything revolves around her because she always gets herself into dumb situations, but Kareem was always to rescue her. That same brother she felt didnt give her enough attention was the one always right there when needed.

"I thought we agreed that if we didnt tell Kareem about that boy hitting you again, and busting out my window that you would stop associating yourself with him." Carol said, slightly annoyed. Lauren thought she was slick, and now she was trying to get one over on her and Carol didnt like that. She was trying to save her ass from Kareem's wrath but it seemed like Lauren wanted to be yelled and fussed at.

Lauren groaned. "I dont know what your talking about." She lied, picking up a sleeping Aubrey. "Bitch yo stupid ass know what the fuck she talking abou- T'su muther fucking niya!" Carol yelled, and T'suniya let out a huff of furstration. She was trying to be quiet but Lauren just irritates her.

"Like I said I dont know what she talking about!" Lauren repeated, glaring at T'suniya and she was lucky she was holding Aubrey. Or T'suniya would have made her fly into the dresser.

Carol shook her head, she was getting too old to be dealing with this shit. "Lauren, just put Aubrey down and think of something else if you want to leave here. Because ion wantchu going back wit dat bo- Its not about whatchu want! Its about what I want! What Lauren wants!" Lauren yelled, and T'suniya's leg started to shake. She stood up and took Aubrey from Lauren, causing her to furrow her eyebrows but she didnt think nothing of it. Lauren know's T'suniya wouldnt hurt her child.

"Granny just move." Lauren said, pushing her grandma's shoulder to the side and T'suniya shook her head, grabbing Lauren's ponytail and yanking her back. "I know damn well you did not just push granny!" She yelled, slanging her to the ground. Carol sighed. "Ni- Niya let her hair go."

"Marco come get them!" Carol yelled, she did not feel like breaking up a fight. Plus she didnt have the energy.

Marco kept hearing his name being called, causing him to sit up in his bed. "Wea you goi- Ill be right back." Marco said, looking down at Eden and she nodded, turning over.

Marco knew he wasnt supposed to have girls in his granny's house but he brought her in last night, and they both ended up falling asleep while watching movies. When he woke up and seen her he felt like it would be rude to just abruptly kick her out. He and Eden had been talking for a while, and their now good friends.

After putting on a plain white shirt, Marco stepped out of his room closing his bedroom door and walking down the hall to-wards the loud yelling. "Stupid hoe!" T'suniya yelled, slapping the shit out of Lauren. She wasnt going to punch her, even though she wanted to. She just wanted to slap some since into her.

"Oh my gosh!" Marco groaned, walking up to the two. After pulling T'suniya off of Lauren he shook his head looking down at his sister. Extending his hand he waited for her to take it so he could help her stupid ass up, but she slapped his hand away standing herself. "Yea, you needed a ass whoopin." Marco mumbled, before turning to T'suniya who was untouched unbothered. He winked at her and she chuckled causing Lauren to roll her eyes.

She had a relationship with her siblings that Lauren didnt have with them herself, only because she wouldnt allow them to have a cordial relationship with her. She just doesnt see it.

"Who dis lil girl in Marco room!" Henderick yelled, standing in Marco's door frame, holding his cup of coffee. He was coming down the hall and opened the door, all because it's his house. No closed door's in his house, because closed doors clearly lead to babies if you use Lauren for an example.

Carol cut her eyes at Marco, and he rubbed the back of his neck. "Aint it Sunday? Aint we post ta be at church?" He asked, and T'suniya chuckled but her laughing stopped once she seen Carol mugging her. "I told you to calm down and you got to fighting her anyway." Carol said, putting her hands on her hips and T'suniya's jaw dropped. "She pushed you!"

Carol shook her head. "You still gotta control your anger Niya." Carol calmly spoke. Like many other things, thats one thing T'suniya and Kareem had in common. Their temper was something serious, except Kareem can now control his but T'suniya. She dont care who you are or what you say, if she wants to say something she will say it and if she feels like you need to be slapped around a couple times then she'll slap you around a few times.

T'suniya sighed. "Marco got a girl in his room." She said, to get the attention off of her and Marco smacked his lips. "Damn. Its like dat Niya?" He asked, holding his arms out and T'suniya shurgged.

"Marco Lamont Jhonson!" Carol yelled, cutting her eyes at him. From what she was thinking, she was disappointed. "Granny I swear it aint nun going on like dat." Marco truthfully spoke and Carol sighed, she was annoyed because she be-lieved him. Even though she didnt want to. "Go get her...let me see ha." Carol said, waving him off and Marco smiled, kissing her cheek before walking out the room.

# Chapter 13

------------------------------------------------------------

The sound of Dove's ringing phone woke her up, and she slightly turned reaching for it on the nightstand as Kareem's grip on her waist tightened. Dove mentally cursed herself out, seeing the time read four thirty.

"Who calling you so early?" Kareem asked, voice muffled from his face being in the pillow. "Nobody.." Dove replied, quickly sending her momma a text. Once the text went through she hopped out the bed, and Kareem looked up with a mug on his face. "Dove what the fuck is you doing. Getcho ass back in dis be- Dont you got work?" She asked, putting on some basketball shorts. Which were Kareem's.

Kareem sat up, wiping his eyes. "Naw Ian got work, its Sunday. Whatchu doing allat fo?" He asked, watching her frantically walk around the room picking up and throwing shit away.

Sunday, the day her parents come to check up on her. When really they just want to see if she had been around Kareem.

"Kareem I need you to do me a favor.." Dove finally spoke, standing in the middle of her dorm in a tanktop and Kareems shorts. Kareem looked at her, with worry all over his face. "You good? Was going on?" He asked, hoping everything was ok. He'd hate to have to beat somebody's ass and he just woke up.

"Can you put this hoodie on and..leave?" She asked, and his expression quickly changed to a mug. "What the fuck you mean leave?" He asked, with a little chuckle. She got to be joking.

Dove was scared and to say she wasnt would be a lie. Actually she was beyond scared. For her father to walk into this room and see Kareem, shirtless in her bed. Would be a nightmare of her's.

It hurts Dove that she cant just explain to Kareem her situation, its been so many days where she's wanted to vent to him but something wont let her. She doesnt want him to look at her any different.

"Kareem can you just put it on!" Dove said, her voice slightly raising and he plainly looked at her, it was something going on but he couldnt put his finger on it. He stood up and she backed up a little bit, which he noticed.

"Was wrong witchu?" He asked, slowly stepping towards her and she shook her head, holding the hoodie out to him while looking every where but at him.

"Why you not looking at me?" He asked, touching her chin and tilting her head up to look into his eyes, and she quickly backed up, continuing to look around her. She kept going in and out of flashbacks, and usually when that would happen she'd be by herself.

A knock on the door caused her to flinch, and Kareem held her body as her breathing quickened. Kareem couldnt believe it, how didn't he notice. This was the same shit Lauren used to do.

"Put dis on and go out da window." Dove spoke, her voice steady and calm but her nerves sky high. "Dov- Come open the door Dove!" Tasha yelled, knocking again.

Kareem stepped back, chuckling. "You for real? You tryna get me ta leave cause yo peoples coming?" He asked and Dove once again sighed. "Kareem I swear its not m- You ashamed of me?" He asked, and she covered her face, taking deep breaths. "Kareem you dont understa- Then explain!" He yelled, and she looked up mugging him. "What am I supposed to say!" She yelled back, and Tasha raised her eyebrows confused.

"Who the hell is she talking to?" Tasha asked Nathan and he shook his his with a mug. "I feel like I know who." He grumbled, banging on the door. "Dove open this damn door!" He yelled. Just wait until he got in this room. She was gonna learn her lesson.

"Jus please go.." Dove said, feeling the tears coming. Now she fucked up with Kareem, again! Plus, her father was gonna beat her ass. Kareem swiped a hand down his face, finally piecing everything together. One of her parents is abusing her, obviously her daddy from what he seen that one day. Kareem didnt want to leave her, he wanted to beat her fathers ass then sit and have a talk with Dove. Why didnt she tell him?

"Listen, Dove ian finna leave y- Just get the fuck out Kareem!" Dove yelled, hearing the door knob shake. Tasha had forgot she got a key, so they could pop in whenever they'd like.

Kareem went to say something but he silenced himself, nodding. "Dis was yo last time Dove." He pointed, before going towards the door.

Dove looked to the ceiling, feeling the tears roll down her cheeks. Why did she constantly push him away? All she wanted to do was be free. She felt like a caged bird, every time she'd find happiness her parents fucked it up.

Just as the door opened, Kareem brushed past Nathan and when Nathan went to go after him Tasha quickly grabbed her husbands arm. "We dont want a repeat of last time.." She whispered, ushering him into the room and Nathan yanked his arm away from her before walking into the dorm and Tasha followed. Closing the door, and being sure to lock it. She knew what was about to happen...

Dove's hands went to her fathers trying to pull them from around her neck. "Nathan dont kill he- Shut up!" He yelled, and Tasha backed up a little. Frowning at the sight of Dove losing oxygen. She wasnt as bad as Nathan, but that didnt make her better.

"You fucking dat boy?" Nathan asked, loosening his grip just a little and Dove shook her head. "You lying ta me?" Nathan asked, and she slowly shook her head, becoming light headed.

He threw her to the ground and she landed with a thud, gasping for air before letting out coughs. The next thing she knew, there was an excruciating pain in her stomach, and Nathan continued to kick her. She didnt yell, she didnt cry, she just lied there. If she would've put up a fight he would have saw it as a challenge, and beat her worse.

Kareem was mugging anybody in sight. He was pissed and all he wanted to do was beat somebody's ass. As he said, that was her last time fucking over him and they arn't even together. He wasnt finna take shit from a female that he hasnt claimed and not been claimed by.

Obviously it was something up but if she didnt tell him, he cant do nothing about it. He has too much on the line to be risking it all on thoughts and assumptions.

Just as he made it to his building, his phone rang and he sighed before fixing his attitude and accepting the call. "Wassup grams?" He spoke, sound happy enough.

He stood there frozen as he listened to his grandmother speak.

"Im on my way."

# Chapter 14

"**W**ea she at?"

Everybody looked up, hearing that familiar voice. Kareem stood in his grandmother's living room throwing his bags, not caring where they landed.

Keyonna's face lit up and she went to run to her brother but T'suniya grabbed her arm, seeing Kareem's facial expression. "I dont think he want no hug right no- No! move!" Keyonna yelled, getting herself out of T'suniya's grip and running to her brother.

Kareem adjusted his facial expression, reaching down and picking her up. Now with a smile on his face. "Wassup Kee." He greeted her and she layed her head on his chest. "I misted you."

He rubbed her back, walking into the kitchen. "Wea ha ass at?" Kareem asked, and Carol sighed. "Woke up this morning, and she was gone.."

"She must have heard granny talking to you." Marco said, eating a spoon of fruit loops. Kareem shook his head. He dont know why she running, cause he gone find her. "Was dis I hear bout you having somebody up in granny house?" He asked, growing a smirk. Trying to relax his nerves.

Marco smacked his lips, growing a smile of his own and everybody stared at him. "Ha name Eden." He started, and everyone payed attention, except Keyonna whom fell asleep in her brothers comforting arms. She missed him a lot, seeing everything that was going on was kind of scary.

"She brown skin, short hair, fine as hell n she smart." Marco said, continuing to smile at the thought of his friend. "She does seem like a sweet girl." Carol added, nodding her head and Kareem nodded.

"Bet not be fucking no lil girls in my granny house." Kareem warned and Marco scrunched his face up. "You used to sneak Malina in!" He yelled, pursing his lips together and T'suniya made the duck lip's face, raising her eyebrows.

Henderick chuckled. "You a sly lil nigga. I like dat!" He said, dapping Kareem up and they laughed as Carol glared at them.

"Kareem you snuck a lil girl in my hous- I gotta go find Lauren. Mhm, yep." Kareem said, standing up and everybody laughed, including Carol.

After he put Keyonna in her bed, he walked to the front of the house and Marco followed him outside. "Wat happened to lil lady you had on da phone dat day? I thought she woulda came witchu." Marco said, hopping into their grandfathers cadilac.

Kareem got in too. "I thought it coulda been some, but naw." He said, starting the car and Marco nodded, not wanting to press him on it.

"Reem, dont do nun stupid. We going to get ha n we leaving. We dont need you getting back locked up." Marco said, leaning back in the seat and Kareem nodded. "Ill try..." He mumbled, backing out of the driveway.

Anthony shook his head, pacing back and forth. "You finna lead them niggas right to me!" He yelled, staring at Lauren as she looked down at her hands. "I didnt know wea else ta go!" She yelled, looking up at him and she ended up on the floor, holding the cheek he just slapped.

"I got a bitch finna come ova hea so you gone have ta leave. You coulda went any damn wea! N you gone come hea. Are you dumb?" Anthony asked, looking down at her, as she silently cried.

"You cant hea or some?" He asked and she closed her eyes, at this point she wanted to forget everything and everybody. Fear shot through out her body, as she felt the aching pain in her stomach. "Ahhh!" She yelped out in pain as he kicked her again. He knelt down beside her, smirking. "So sound do come from yo mouth." He said, smirking and she felt the tears rolling down her cheeks as she held her stomach. If he loved her, he would regret that. But he doesnt.

"Slow down Ree- I just heard ha yell!" Kareem yelled, busting in the small home.

The sight caused him to lose his mind.

"He's gonna kill him!" Lauren yelled, trying to get out of Marco's grip. "Lauren sto- No! What about Aubrey!" Lauren continued to yell, watching her brother beat the love of her life. She was starting to think the beatings he gave her wasnt so bad, maybe she could have done something different, she was filled with guilt. Like it was her fault he was being killed, because technically it is.

Just an inch of Anthony's life, the cries of Aubrey snapped Kareem out of whatever he was in. He quickly stepped back, looking down at himself, seeing all the blood on his clothes and hands brought back bad memories. Marco let go of Lauren so he could check up on Kareem, but Kareem shook his head, hearing his footsteps behind him and Marco stopped, going to grab Aubrey instead.

Kareem watched as Lauren clung to Anthony's body, with wet cheek's from her tears. Kareem sniffed. He couldnt save her in the beginning and he knew it, now he was tired of saving her. "Dont." He started, catching her attention. "Eva ask me fo shit else, cause I promise you." He sniffed. "I will come running, and that'll get me killed or in jail. So, if you love me like I love you." He continued, wiping his tears not caring about the blood on his hands. "Dont ask me fo shit else." He finished, pointing at her before walking away.

"Kareem..." She called, feeling the tears roll down her cheeks, once again. "Kareem I- im sorry!" She yelled, standing up. Stepping out the house Kareem sighed, leaning on his grandfathers car.

Marco held Aubrey and her thing's, going towards the door. "Marco wea is you going wit her? Wea you taking h- Granny gone take care of her." Marco said, continuing towards the door and Lauren shook her head, following him. "You cant take my daughter!" She yelled, stepping out of the house.

"Karee- Marco you cant take her! She is my daughter!" Lauren yelled, trying to take Aubrey out of Marco's arm's but he nudged her so he could put Aubrey in the car. Everybody knew Lauren wasnt gonna be able to care for Aubrey, especially with Anthony around.

Kareem watched Lauren cry and his heart was continuing to break. He couldnt watch, so he went around the car and got in the drivers seat. Pulling out his phone there was only one person he could call.

"Please..." She begged, watching Marco strap Aubrey into the car seat. Lauren some how found herself on the ground, crying. Her whole world was falling apart. Not only did she lose her family but she lost two children.

She's sure the pain she felt when Anthony was kicking her stomach didnt mean her baby's ok.

All over a man who doesnt give a damn about her, damn...

# Chapter 15

Malina watched as Kareem pulled his pants on, in silence. After grabbing his phone and grandfather's keys, Kareem went to walk out of her bedroom. "So thats it?" Malina asked, with a scrunched up face as she sat up in her bed. Kareem sighed, turning around to face her. "Whatchu want?" He asked, holding his arms out.

"So you came over hea just to fuck me?" She asked, cutting her eyes at him and Kareem chuckled. "I came ova hea to talk to somebody who knew bout da shit I go through, you was da one touching on me. Being all freaky n shit, so. You got watchu wanted n I still aint got da shit I needed off my chest." He truthfully spoke, shrugging.

"Well, lets talk..." Malina said, pulling the sheet over her body and patting beside her, suggesting for Kareem to sit down. Kareem stood there looking at his high school girlfriend, before shaking his head. "Ion wanna talk no mo." He told her, with a head nod before walking out of her bedroom.

Some people just dont change, and Malina hasnt. Her affect on him hasnt either. Back in high school, whenever he needed to talk about something he'd always go to her and most of the time he knew it was because they'd end up having sex but now, this time. He really needed an old friend to talk to, but just like back then he always gave in.

After exiting Malina's apartment, Kareem got into his grandfather's Cadillac taking in a long breath, then exhaling. Out of everything going on in his life. All he could think about was her, the realization of what could have happened to her when he left caused him to pull his phone out, ignoring the time that read three in the morning. He clicked her name, biting his bottom lip.

As he waited for her to answer his nerves only got worse, this was his third time calling. Any other time she wouldnt let it get to the third ring.

He clicked on the contact that read Ugly ass hoping at least she picked up.

"Wassup lil nigga." Gia greeted him, making a left in her white impala heading towards a nice apartment building. "Yo, wea you at?" Kareem asked, leaning back in his seat. "Da car, obviously." She responded, motioning around her. They were on facetime so he could clearly see.

"Wea you headed I mean?" He asked and Gia smacked her lips. "Nigga, ian no child. Youn gotta know wea im goi- Wea da fuck yo ugly ass going?" Kareem cut her off, not caring about nothing else she had to say. "Bitch since you wanna know so mutha fucking bad! Im going to get my cat ate!" Gia yelled, rolling her neck and Kareem scrunched his face up.

"Exactly. Shoulda minded yo business." Gia told him, pulling up at her sneaky link location. "Wea you at?" Gia asked, taking her seatbelt off and Kareem shook his head. She talk too much.

"My peoples house." He said, and she nodded. "What did you call me fo? Cause dese links be timed. I gotta get in hea fo my sugga momma husband come home." Gia said, pursing her lips together and Kareem shook his head. She just wild.

"Oh!" He remembered, his nerves getting bad again. "I need you ta go check on Dove." He said, and she nodded. "Ok ill go tomor- Naw like right now, I gotta feeling some aint right.." He said and Gia groaned buckling again. "You lucky she my bitch cause, I was finna get a burkin bag."

Kareem waved her off. "Call me soon as you reach da building." He said and Gia smirked. "Call me soon as you reach da buil- ol simp ass." Gia chuckled and Kareem smacked his lips, hanging up the phone.

Gia finally arrived on campus. She exited her car, putting some pep in her step as she went towards Dove's building. She thought Kareem was over exaggerating but when she called herself and Dove didnt answer, Gia became nervous herself.

She tried to take the time of night into consideration but she knows that Dove doesnt care what time it is, if a friend is calling she'll answer.

Gia was even more nervous when she remembered that Dove had called her a couple hours ago, but she was sleep so she decided she'd call her back once she got up, since her sneaky link had been planned already she knew she'd be up in soon time, but she forgot to call.

Clicking on the name Lil Nigga in her contact's Gia slid her student access key, before opening the glass door and stepping into Dove's building.

Hearing the little sound, Gia looked down seeing Kareem had answered the facetime call. "Im hea.." She said, stepping up to Dove's door. "Aight, she good?" Kareem asked, before taking another drag from the backwood, he got from Marco.

"Ion know n youn post ta be smoking. You on da basketball tea- Just see if she good Gia." Kareem said, putting the wood in the ashtray and Gia rolled her eyes, raising her fist to the door to knock but when she touched it, the door slightly moved. Which let her know it was open.

"The door open...Im scared Kareem." Gia whispered, as she slowly stepped into the dark room. Kareem sighed, trying to shake all bad thoughts. "Her people probably left the door open." He suggested and Gia nodded, as she looked around until seeing the little crack of light coming from the bathroom. The door was almost completely closed but just a little open.

"Da bathroom light on." Gia said and Kareem smacked his lips. "Go in dea den." He told her, while shaking his head. She was blowing his high acting slow.

Gia ignored the tone in his voice, knowing this isnt the time to argue.

She pushed the bathroom door, stepping in she instantly dropped her phone and ran over to the bath tub. "What happened!" Kareem yelled, and Gia felt tears on her cheek's as she looked down at Dove in the bathtub full of water, passed out.

There was pill bottles all around, but no pills in sight. "I think she overdosed and she got a lot of bruises and she in da bathtub!" Gia yelled, picking her phone back up. She didnt know what to do.

"Ok, first of all calm down." Kareem instructed, swiping a hand down his face. "You gone hang up n call da police den dont touch shit, dont do shit." He continued and Gia nodded. "Why cant I touc- Cause dey gone try ta pin some on you. You wanna go ta jail?" He asked and she shook her head. "Aight den, now hurry up! Youn know how long she been dea." He said, and Gia hung the phone up following his instrustions.

Kareem threw his phone in the passenger seat, starting the car.

All he was thinking about was if he hadda stayed.

# Chapter 16

Looking out the small round window of the spirit airplane, Kareem sighed as he observed the cloud's and the sun coming up for the morning. It's a beautiful sight, pink, purple, and blue along with the orange hue from the sun.

"Aight Dove, imma need you ta pull through.." He whispered, only to where he could hear himself. Not even Marco could hear him, and he was right beside him. Marco wanted to go to Mentone with Kareem for moral support. He didnt know what Kareem and Dove's relationship was but judging by how his brother hasnt said one word, nor ate anything in hours. It has to be something real.

"The time is six o' two, the weather's quite nice today at sixty degree's. We have arrive in Mentone and were landing in ten. Please buckle up, all tables up and brace yourself for landing, thank you." The pilot spoke, over the intercom and shuffling was heard as everyone followed his directions.

Marco looked over to his brother with a worried expression of his own. "She gone be good." Marco said, not expecting a response and he didnt get one.

After claiming their bags, Marco and Kareem headed for the glass double doors leading out of the airport. Luckily, their uber was already there. Kareem sat in the passenger seat, while Marco sat in the back. "How yall doing?" The older man asked and to Marco's surprise Kareem sent him a head nod. "Good n you?" Marco responded, pulling his phone out. "Im as good as ill be, where too?" The man asked, cranking up the car. Marco clicked Eden's name on his phone before looking up as he spoke. "Novil Hospital."

The driver nodded before heading in that direction.

Eden finally answered the phone and Marco smiled. "Took yo ass long enough." He said, looking out the window at the beautiful city. It looks nothing like dirty ol Crato Bay. "Boy shut the fuck up." Eden said, rolling her eyes as she passed her little brother a plate with his breakfast on it. If Eden couldnt do nothing, she could cook.

"Ion like ya tone ms mam." Marco said, leaning back in the seat. Eden sat at the table with her brother. "Whatever Lamont." She said, smirking as she popped a grape in her mouth. Marco smacked his lips, with a small smile. She must have heard Carol say his full name. "Dont start Eden Shanell Price." Marco replied, seeing them come up on the hospital.

Eden chuckled. "But ay, imma call you lata." Marco said, taking his seatbelt off. Eden's smile slightly faltered. She didnt want to get off the phone. "Ok. Be safe ugly." Eden said, before sipping from her orange juice. Marco smirked. He could hear the sadness in her voice. "Bye ugly." He responded, before hanging up.

After grabbing their bags which was a duffle bag each, being that Kareems stuff was back in his dorm and Marco isnt staying long. The boys entered the hospital, just as Kareem's phone vibrated in his pocket.

He pulled it out seeing a text from Gia.

Ugly ass: You here yet?

Kareem looked around him, not feeling the environment as he typed.

Lil Nigga: yea

Gia let out a sigh of relief, she felt all alone and even though she didnt talk about it much. She really cares about Kareem and Dove, like their her siblings.

Ugly ass: She good

Kareem covered his mouth, staring down at the phone. The hot tears on his cheeks caused him to sniff as he wiped them away. He let out a breath he didnt even know he was holding in as he looked up to the ceiling. "You good br- She' good." Kareem said, a big smile appearing on his face and Marco smiled. Patting his brothers back he pulled him along. "Lets go see her den, dafuck we standing hea fo!" Marco yelled, catching some peoples eye but the brothers ignored them approaching the front desk.

"Dove Dasani." Kareem said, his smile still on his face. He was so happy his cheeks were starting to hurt. The receptionist smiled, before typing on her desktop. "Room One fifteen." She said, and the boy's rushed to the elevator causing her to chuckle.

Gia was uncomfortable, Tasha and Nathan kept sending her these weird looks. But she didnt care how much they looked at her funny, she wasnt leaving Dove's side. Espicially knowing what they do to her, their probably the ones who gave her all those bruises.

Gia felt like they thought looking at her funny would make her leave the room, for whatever reason but she wasnt leaving.

"Im not comfortable being in here." Nathan mumbled, Gia saw their mouths moving but she couldnt hear them.

"You had one fucking job, drug her and make it look like a damn overdose situation." Nathan continued and Tasha rolled her eyes. "Im tired of doing thi- Oh well, were ridding the world of their kind." Nathan cut in, causing her to go silent.

Now, Nathan planned to just smother her with a pillow being that she's asleep but this bitch wont leave the room. He'd be dammed if he was to get caught, he hasnt gotten caught before and he didnt plan on starting now because of one girl's group of nigga friends.

"We should just leave, let the girl live the rest of her lif- Dammit Tasha!" Nathan yelled, catching Gia's attention and her grip on Dove's hand tightened. "Were not leaving until the job is done!" Nathan yelled, and Tasha sighed, seeing Gia watching them.

"Lower your tone." Tasha calmly said, hoping that would calm him down but it didnt. "We should just kill her too!" Nathan yelled, and Gia's eyes grew big. Never letting go of Dove's hand, Gia reached down beside her with her left hand grabbing the small Gucci clutch purse from her sugga momma.

Taking the light pink taser out she hid it behind her back. Taking deep breaths she turned her attention back to a sleeping Dove.

"Nathan I said lower your ton- Mentone PD!" The officers yelled, busting in the small room, causing Dove to jump out of her sleep and Gia rubbed her arm, relaxing her as they both watched the scene before them.

Tasha and Nathan were being handcuffed and told their rights, while being escorted out of the room.

Kareem and Marco stepped off the elevator, which got stuck for a good ten minutes but finally they were off. "This is all your fault!" Nathan yelled, and Tasha ignored him as she balled her eyes out. "Damnnnnnn." Marco dragged, seeing all the police just for those two people.

"Das Doves parents!" Kareem said, pointing as they stepped to the side allowing the officers and Tasha and Nathan to get on the elevator. "You for real?" Marco asked, and Kareem nodded. "Lets go see wassup." He said, rushing down the hall and Marco followed. Shit like this never happened in Crato Bay, maybe his hood wasnt so bad.

"What are they being charged for exactly?" Dove managed to ask the officer, it felt weird for her to talk but she was ok. Kareem and Marco entered the room causing Gia to smile. She waved and Kareem walked over to her, as she stood. Without any word's Gia and Kareem embraced each other in a warm and comforting ugly. "Yo ugly ass bet not start crying." Kareem said, and Gia smacked her lips. "Boy bye, ion cry over nigga's. But you, maybe ill shed a lil tear." She joked, causing everybody to laugh a little, even the officer.

They pulled back from the hug, hearing the officer speak. "Their being charged with first degree murder, child kidnapping, robbery, identity theft, sex trafficking, and much more." The officer spoke, keeping his natural expression as everyone looked at him in shock, except Dove. She wasnt surprised that they could do all that, judging by how they treated her.

"Let me explain." The officer started. "They are known as the One fifteen couple and ill tell you why. When's your birthday?" The officer asked Dove and swallowed before speaking. "January fifteenth..."

"Sad to tell you, but no it isnt. Thats why their called the One fifteen couple. They would take black newborn babies from room one fifteen, from the most popular hospital in the city their in. Then raise them, abusing them and downing them until they decided they were ready to move and start again. In all the cases we have, the kid has ended up dead. But not you...your lucky." The officer nodded, and everyone was silent so he decided to continue speaking.

"Every police department has been tracking them for years. The people you know as Tasha and Nathan have been Regina and Sean, Natalie and Robert, Amanda and Adam, plus many, many more..." The officer concluded, with a sigh and Dove cleared her throat. "How many kids?"

"Twelve before you..." The officer informed her and she sighed.

"Their al- Dead." The officer nodded, and she went quiet.

Gia frowned. "They were all black?" She asked, and everyone looked her way. "Yea....they saw it as their way of ridding the world of our kind.." The officer said, and Gia looked down at her shoes.

"What was their names?" Marco asked, sitting up straight from his seat on the couch.

The officer wasnt supposed to be sharing this information, but it was something about this group of kids that made him want to keep talking. "The twelve dead are Aria, Brooke, Calla, Carson, James, Enrick, Haley, Zaniya, Ivy, William, Jerome and Masani. The one alive is A- "

"Arcaida Jackson." A beautiful high yellow woman spoke, entering the room and everybody stared at her. "Her name is

Arcaida Danice Jackson and she was taken from me on September fifth at one fifteen in the morning, from room one fifteen." The woman truthfully spoke, wiping her tears that fell as she stared at her daughter, Arcaida.

Dove felt the tears burning down her cheeks as she sat up, and Mae Jackson embraced her daughter in a needed, comforting hug as Dove cried. "Momma..." She sobbed, holding on tight to the woman she only just met, but felt like she knew for years.

"I gotchu Cai..."

# Chapter 17

"I should be heading home.." Mae said, standing from the couch and Dove's smile faltered. The two had been talking for hour's, and the conversation seemed like it could go on forever but Mae does have work in the morning and the hospital said Dove was set to leave hours ago.

Walking over to Arcaida, Mae smiled. She look's a lot like her when she was younger. The heart shaped lips, light brown eye's, mid length eye lashes. She's beautiful.

"How would you like to meet a couple people?" Mae asked, and Dove raised her eyebrows. "Meet who?" She asked, sitting up in the bed. "Your father and brother." Mae bluntly stated, she wanted Travis and Camden to come with her earlier but Travis refused. He was tired of having false hope, any black girl that came into the hospital they were trying to say it was their daughter just to push off their case but Travis wasn't gonna get disappointed this time. So him and eight year old Camden stayed home, eating pizza and watching football.

Travis knew his baby girl was out there, where? He didnt know but he knew she was close by. He could feel it.

He beat himself up about it everyday, he was supposed to protect her, keep her out of harms way, teach her how to talk, and walk, teach her to know her worth and much more. But, he never got the chance. After Mae had given birth, the nurse Tasha Dasani came in to take Arcaida for her check up, being that she was a few months late she claimed that the hospital wanted to make sure she was ok, and there was no signs of illness. But, she never came back.

Of course they had seen Tasha around the hospital, or else they wouldnt have let her take their child. She had a uniform and everything, she was actually apart of the staff. All that, just to take their child.

Dove's eyes grew big along with her smile. "I have a brother?" She asked, feeling herself grow excited. Dove alway's wanted siblings and she was often lonely. "Yea, wanna see him?" Mae asked, pulling her phone out seeing Dove nod.

After pulling up a picture of Travis and Camden, Mae passed Dove the phone and her face lit up. "He's so cute.." Dove whispered, smiling at the picture. Camden is the spitting image of Travis. The same lips, eyes, and nose. The only thing it seemed that Camden got from Mae was her light brown eye's, because he even has Travis's brown skin complexion.

Their hair was even alike, they both have waves. Well, Camden's arnt waves just yet, maybe ripples.

"How soon can I meet them?" Dove asked, passing her mother her phone back. She was ready to start her new life, new family, new profession, new her...

The one thing she wanted to keep, was her friends. Though she only has two, thats all she needs.

The thought of Kareem, caused her to look down at her finger's. She noticed him walk in the room earlier but she was too overwhelmed by the situation in front of her to speak to him.

"We can have dinner whenever your ready, I just know Travis is gonna love to hear about this." Mae nodded, about to click her phone off but stopping herself. "Is there any number I can get to get in contact with you?" She asked, hoping Dove would say yes, she'd hate to lose contact with her and she just found her.

"Im gonna buy a new phone so- You can have my numba, ill let ha know if you called. Until she gets ha own." Kareem said, stepping into the room. "I told yo stupid ass to wait!" Gia yelled, coming in behind him. Holding the Popeyes they purchased hours ago. "Man we been sitting out dere fo hours, n I bet dat food cold now." Marco said, yawning and taking a good stretch. "Ooowee. Both yall can suck my dick. N yep, I got one." Gia said, placing the food on a rolling tray before stepping back out the room.

It is true, they had been sitting outside the room for hours because Gia told them to wait a while. When they first arrived they heard the laughing and lively conversation Mae and Dove were having, so they did decide to let them continue having their moment.

In that time, Dove had learned that her father was in the military from eighteen to twenty six. Until he became the coach for the Mentone Bearcats football team. Then she learned her mother was a well known chef, Owning a few of the top restaurants in Mentone. It wasnt easy for the couple of twelve years, they had their own adversities. But in the end they thought everything would be ok, until their daughter was taken from them. They kept hope, while trying to continue on with their lives but sometimes hope could die, they'd just revive it.

"Ok.." Mae nodded, passing her phone to the handsome young man and he smiled, typing his number in before giving her the phone back. "Well, Ill see you soon. Ok?" Mae said, leaning in and embracing Arcaida in a strong and comforting hug. "Im looking forward too it." She responded, holding on to her mother.

After pulling back from the hug, the two woman held smiles on their beautiful faces. Happy was an understatement. Once Mae left the room, Marco followed behind her sensing some kind of tension between Dove and his brother. Plus he wanted to call Eden anyway.

Marco looked around the hall, wondering where Gia had went since she wasnt outside the room. He wasnt gonna worry about it for long, since his call with Eden was on the second ring but she answered on the third. On the other hand, Gia wasnt worried about them no more, since she found out everybody was ok she was back to her normal and regular self. Now, she was trying to find the cute receptionist.

Sitting down on the couch, Kareem sighed looking down at his hands. The past seventy two hours was a lot for him, but he kept it pushing being that he really had no time to sit and reflect. Everything was happening back to back. Then the little time he got to actual sit, his mind was always taken over by something causing his nerves to get bad.

"The beating's happened for as long as I can remember..." She started, taking a quick deep breath. She couldnt believe it, she was finally gonna do it. "If I didnt obey them, that was my punishment even for the little things. Their families hated me, and I used to have to get jumped by Nathan's nephews every holiday. Did they know? Yes, but they felt as though if they hit me they were hitting me for a reason and they were. They didnt like the fact that I wasnt like their other cousin's, they said..." She sighed. "They said I wasnt pretty like all the other girls, so they were gonna literately beat my face." She wiped her cheeks. "That joke wasnt even funny..." She mumbled.

"As I got older, I started to do more of what they expected, and things got better. Until I started to talk about music and R and B. They thougt that kind of music wasnt good, and they said that music wasnt a good route for me anyway, since I so called couldnt sing..." She sighed once again. "Enough about them. Thing will be better now..." Dove nodded, convincing herself of what she just said and she finally looked up to see Kareem standing beside her.

She went to speak but he had already started talking. "I had my mind on one thing going to dat school." He started, sitting beside her and taking her hand into his. "Den hea go dis fine ass girl, all smart and shit. She got dat vibe dat just make you wanna smile every moment you around ha.." He chuckled, rubbing the back of her hand with his thumb. "Shy, and pretty. Dem two dont mix fa me, cause if you pretty I think you should flaunt it. Own dat shit. But yean have nobody to tell you dat huh?" He asked, now looking into her eyes and she couldnt find words to say.

"When somebody dont get da right amount of attention from the people they crave it from, they either put on dis mask of happiness or dey do something to try and get the attention they want. Just in the wrong way. I- I got somebody who did the opposite of whatchu did.." Kareem admitted. "She my heart, ill die fo dat girl. But our father's mistake made my efforts be shadowed. He left, I stepped up. But, no matter what I did, she was spiraling down." He sighed, wiping his eyes and Dove's expression softened. "Shit aint get betta when our momma dood started hitting on her, ian even know. Cause I wasnt neva home. I was always some wea playing ball. I was tryna betta myself to betta our future n my siblings at home getting beat...wit our momma sitting dere, watching.." He ended with a slow nod.

"But ay, guess what." He lowly said, looking into her eyes again and Dove raised an eyebrow.

"I gotchu.." His grip on her hand tightened.

"N I gotchu.." She responded, growing a small smile. "Fo how long?" He asked, fully turning towards her and she looked at him confused. "Whatchu mean?" She asked.

He licked his lips continuing to stare at her. "You said you got me, but just to be sure. Imma need you to answer yes to this question im finna ask you." He seriously spoke. He had already told her, the last time she was gonna fuck over him had past, so if he was gonna take another chance on her he wanted her to be his, for sure.

"Dov- If your going to ask me what I think your about to ask me, use my real name..." She said, keeping eye contact. "Arcaida Danice Jackson." Kareem smiled, seeing her smile at the way he said her first name. It was like it rolled off his tongue. "Be my bitch." He joked, and they bust out laughing.

Arcaida shook her head with a smirk. He couldnt be serious for more than thirty minutes and if he started being goofy she was gonna fall in line. "Aight, aight for real.." He said, getting himself together.

"Arca- " He bust out laughing, and she slapped his arm laughing too. "Come on Reem!" She yelled, and he continued to laugh before taking a deep breath. After calming himself down, he looked back to her and she smiled causing him to laugh again. "Kareem wha- "

She was interrupted by his lips touching her's and and he climbed onto the bed, deepening the kiss. Once he pulled back he smirked at Arcaida's shocked expression. "Yo lips was dry." He shrugged, hovering over and she smiled, kissing him again.

"So you do want to be my girlfriend?" He asked, in between the kiss and she nodded. "Of course." She responded, wrapping her arms around his neck. "You getting a lil touc- " He raised an eyebrow as she reached to take his shirt off. "Naw you playing." He said, before seeing her with the same sly smirk.

What the hell got into her.

"You want me to fuck you?" He asked, getting excited and she smacked her lips. "Boy stop acting dumb, you finna kill my mood." She said, pulling his shirt over his head. Smiling at his abb's and tattoo's. "You a lil frea- Kareem shut up!" Arcaida yelled, he was dead ass about to kill her mood.

"Im just saying, who fuck in da hospita- Is we boutta fuck or no?" Arcaida asked, plainly staring at him and he chuckled before kissing her neck, she grinned biting her bottom lip as her hands traced his back.

# Chapter 18

------------------------------------------------

"Five mo minut- No Kareem. Get up or im leaving you." Arcaida said, throwing the pillow she used to hit Kareem beside him on his bed. She walked over to his desk, searching for her lip gloss, she moved his book's and her make-up and hair products all around. Still not finding it. Groaning she, covered her face clearly annoyed.

Kareem looked over at her before sighing and sitting up. "Was da issue?" He asked, swiping a hand down his face. "Not hing.." Arcaida mumbled, letting her arms hang as she walked into the small bathroom. Finding her lip gloss on the counter she let out a sigh of releif before picking up the tube, and applying the clear gloss.

Kareem leaned in the bathroom's door frame, rubbing his exposed stomach as he yawned. Arcaida went to put her hair up and he furrowed his eyebrows. "Why you doing dat?" He asked, and she raised an eyebrow. "Doing what?"

"Putting yo hair up, yean did that in a minute." Kareem said, as he observed his beautiful girlfriend. Arcaida sighed, taking the bun down so she could redo it. "I want to look..nice." She mumbled, shrugging. Her mood wasnt the best, it seemed like every little thing was getting her down and Kareem for sure noticed.

"You look good witcho hair down, be looking fine as fuck." He complimented her, causing her face to light up. "Thank you.." She mumbled, all of a sudden feeling shy. That's one thing about Kareem, even though their now in a relationship he still gives her butterflies.

He smiled, seeing her mood slightly change. "Naw dont get shy now!" He said, coming up behind her and her smile only grew bigger.

Holding one arm around her waist, he kissed her exposed neck causing her to giggle. She was completely oblivious to what he was actually doing. She felt herself relaxing in his touch, as she tilted her head to give him more access.

It didnt take long for her to snap out of it, being that she remembered her plans for today, and the reason why she was so frantic. "Kareem, come on for real. You gotta get dressed." She seriously spoke, it shouldn't take long for him to get ready, being that they take their showers at night.

Biting his bottom lip, he looked at her through the mirror and she rolled her eyes as he grabbed the hair tie out of her hand. "You might as well wea yo hair down, youn wantcho peoples ta see dem hickeys on ya neck." He told her, with a sly smirk and she mugged him as he grabbed his toothbrush. "Now you know yo stupid ass just did that on purpose!" She yelled, storming out of the bathroom and Kareem chucked, grabbing the Colgate toothpaste. She'll be alright.

Finally arriving at Mae and Travis's home, Arcaida's leg started to shake as her nerves were coming over her. She wasnt nervous to see her mother, it was her father she was scared to see. Obviously being that she has a bad experience with older men, she didnt know how he would react upon seeing her. Kareem rested his hand on her thigh, and the action slightly calmed her down. "Im scared.." She finally admitted and Kareem leaned his head back. "Watchu scaed fo?" He asked, turning off the engine to his grandfathers Cadillac, well now its his Cadillac.

Henderick decided to let Kareem have the car, being that he always payed for the servicing or whatever else it needed, even when he wasnt back in Crato Bay. So, when Marco went back home Kareem flew with him, then drove the car back to Mentone. Did it take a long time? Yes, but he and Arcaida needed some way of transportation besides uber.

"Im scared to see him, what if he tries something or tell's me to get out?" She asked, looking out the window while leaning her head back on the seat. Nervous is an understatement. Kareem sighed. "Watchu mean try som- What if he doesnt want me any more..." she mumbled and Kareem plainly looked at her. "Cai.." He called, and she closed her eyes. She wanted to go back to his dorm and just watch movies. This dinner was causing her to lose control of herself.

"Arcaida." He called, and she closed her legs making him chuckle. "Lil freaky ass." He continued to laugh and she smacked her lips before laughing too.

"For real doe, look at me." He told her, touching her chin and she sighed opening her eyes and looking into his eyes. "Yean neva gotta be scaed, cause imma always be hea. Got me?" He asked, and she nodded. Believing every word he said, because he did indeed mean it. "Gotchu." She replied before unclicking her seat belt and he did the same.

They hopped out the car, and he locked the doors before shoving his keys in the pocket of his black jeans. Him and Arcaida are wearing matching outfits. She chose what they'd wear and Kareem just went along with it. He seen how planning it, helped her mood on that particular day so he just let her do her thing.

"Lemme fix yo collar." Arcaida said, stopping in her tracks and Kareem turned around. "Its cool come on." He said, knowing she was gonna fix it anyway and she did. Arcaida wore a black and fitted dress, with some black flats. She was always wearing heel's and boots. She wanted to do something different. Her dark blue, long and open coat matched Kareem's. Whom was sporting the all black attire as well, with some Jordan one's in the color Royal, along with black and white to match.

He wore his chains, and his left stud. While she wore two stud of her own and a plain silver necklace with the infinity symbol hanging at the end.

Kareem knocked a couple times then Mae answered the door with a smile. "Hey! Come on in." She stepped to the side, allowing the two to enter and Kareem let Arcaida step in before following her.

Mae gave Arcaida a warm hug, before giving Kareem a hug as well. "Ma this is my boyfriend Kareem, im sure you noticed him at the hospital." Arcaida introduced him, and Mae nodded with a smile. "Yes I remember him, and you two look amazing!" She complimented them and they both smiled.

"Thanks." Arcaida thanked her, looking around the house. It was so comforting and inviting.

"Preciate it." Kareem nodded, looking around as well. The house kind of reminded him of his grandmother's place, its just bigger.

A door was opened then closed, and in walked Camden. "Camden wea you just came from?" Mae asked, crossing her arms as she raised an eyebrow. "Outside wit daddy." He pointed, and Mae squinted her eyes. "I mean my room." Camden said, nodding and Kareem chuckled. Once you say some different from the first time they already know you lying.

"Boy I heard dat toilet flush n yo nasty ass aint wash yo hands." Mae said, and Camden sighed. "Not today Mae Jackso- Boy you betta getcho ass in dat bathroom n wash yo hands!"

Mae yelled, going to take her belt off and Arcaida and Kareem chuckled seeing Camden run down the hallway.

"Just embarrassing." Mae chuckled, before turning back to her daughter and her boyfriend. "The food's almost done. But Cai you could help with some little stuff if you'd like."

Arcaida nodded. "For sure, whatchu need help with?" She aksed, placing her purse down and Kareem touched her shoulder, before helping her out of her coat. "Thank you." She thanked him and he nodded. "Gone head n do yo thang." He said, hanging their coats on the rack and she smiled following her mother.

"I got the ribs off da gri- " Travis stopped his sentence, staring at the young girl in his kitchen. He placed the ribs down on his marbled counter, with a shocked expression. "Thats Ca- Yea.." Mae nodded and Travis grew a big smile. "I- " He started to speak before just walking up to her and embracing her in a strong hug. Arcaida smiled trying to hold back tears, while hugging him back.

Kareem smiled, standing in the door frame as he watched the scene before him. "Wassup bitch." Camden greeted Kareem, standing beside him and Kareem bust out laughing. What the hell did he just say?

"Yea..haha. Anyway, Im Cam n from what Im hearing thats my sister." He pointed to Arcaida who was in a what seemed to be a interesting conversation with her parents. "N obviously you ha boyfriend or whateva. So if you hurt my sister. Is gone be me n you!" Camden pointed from him to Kareem, and Kareem grinned.

"Dont let my age fool ya, have a nice evening." Camden finished, patting Kareem's arm before walking towards Arcaida to formaly introduce himself.

Kareem couldnt help but to chuckle again, a damn eight year old just tried to punk him. "Little nigga betta hadda washed his hands, touching me n shit." Kareem mumbled, shaking his head.

"Dad, this is my boyfriend Kareem." Arcaida said, pointing to Kareem and he stood up straight before walking towards them. "Hey how you doing?" Kareem spoke, Shaking Travis hand. Travis indeed did notice the good handshake. "Good and you?" Travis asked, and Kareem shrugged. "Im good."

"Foods ready and the tables set!" Mae yelled from in the dining room, and everyone rushed that way excpet Camden who sighed. "Fat asses.." He mumbled, before making his way in there.

The meal was great, and everyone got along just fine. Except when Camden and Kareem would end up having staring contest. Kareem was annoyed because he kept losing, and Camden saw it as him bitching Kareem, again.

"Imma beatcho lil ass." Kareem said, pointing to Camden and Camden bucked at him. "Keep on." Kareem said, continuing to point at him and everybody chuckled.

"So, Cai. Since you decided you didnt want to sing anymore. What do you want to do?" Travis asked, truly curious. He had learned a lot about his daughter and her boyfriend over these past few hours.

Arcaida plans to get an apartment, so she and Kareem can stop living on campus. Plus she dropped out, so she's just been sleeping in Kareem's dorm. Her passion was never to work in Criminal Justice and she barely sings anymore, so she decided to keep it as a hobby.

"Momma said I could work at one of her restaurants, let me move up in the ranks and then potentially own one." Arcaida said, before eating a fork of greens. She loved her momma's cooking if she didnt like anything else. She was also happy her mother was teaching her how to cook, or else her and Kareem would be starving.

Mae nodded, being that those were her exact words. "Since you dropped out wea you staying?" Mae asked, concerned. She didnt want her to feel like she had to be in a hotel or something.

"With Kareem." Arcaida said, before biting into a rib. "How long yall plan on living on campus?" Travis asked, looking to Kareem. "Not too much longer, in about a week or so ill be pay-ing rent on this apartment near campus, since im still attending school." Kareem informed him, and Travis nodded in approval.

They didnt have it all together, but they werent falling apart either. So, Travis liked the guy his daughter chose to date.

"Whatchu going ta school for again?" Travis asked, drinking from his glass of scotch.

"Sports management." Kareem nodded, and Travis smiled, sitting his glass beside his plate. "Well i'll be dammed, Im the coach for the Mentone Bearcats." He said and Kareem smacked his lips. "I knew I seen you some wea!" Kareem yelled, and Travis nodded. Mae and Arcaida chuckled at how they got so hype, for no reason.

They started talking about football and Arcaida shook her head, not wanting to hear nothing about tackles and touch downs. But overall she was happy her father and boyfriend got along.

She was, Happy.

# Chapter 19

Arcaida put some beans and rice on the glass plate, she held in her left hand before putting two chicken legs beside it. She placed the plate at the small island before turning around and reaching into the steel fridge, and grabbing the minute maid fruit punch she had just bought earlier.

As she poured the juice, she heard the front door open and close. "Cai!" Kareem yelled, stepping into the apartment then closing the door.

"Im right hea." She said, placing the glass of juice on the island before grabbing another glass to make herself a drink. After Kareem took his coat off he walked over to her, with a big smile on his face. "How was yo day?" He asked, pecking her lips and she smiled. "Good, Im doing good at the restaurant and momma said im cooking so good ill be head chef in no time. How was yo day?" She asked, grabbing her cup and sipping some juice.

"It was good but ay dat one professor you used ta say was always mugging you n shit got fired." Kareem said, eating a spoon full of beans and rice as Arcaida's eyes grew big. "Mr Willcox?" She asked and Kareem nodded, enjoying his food.

"Wooow. Now he's Mr Will work for food." Arcaida joked, busting out laughing and Kareem smacked his lips before chuckling a little bit.

Once her laughing simmered down she went to make her a plate then Gia one, since she was coming over for a while.

"Ooo bae, I was thinking we could host a Christmas party! Espicially since we went over my momma house for thanks giving. We could invite your family and my family. Because I still havnt met your's in person ye- " She was interrupted by the sound of kareem's phone ringing and Arcaida turned around to see Kareem wasnt even standing there.

She sat the two prepared plates of food down, before picking up his phone. "Kareem yo phone ringing!' She yelled, looking down at the caller ID. It was an unknown number.

"Answer it!" Kareem yelled, from their bedroom. He was changing into some basketball shorts.

Pressing accept on the call, Arcaida grabbed a fork from their utensil drawer then walking over to her plate. "Hello?" A fe-male voice on the other end of the line spoke, and Arcaida raised an eyebrow. "Hello." She replied.

"Umm..who is this?" The girl asked and Arcaida tilted her head to the side, scooping some beans and rice onto her fork.

"Who is thi- Is Kareem around? I have to tell him something." The girl asked, cutting off Arcaida's sentence.

So she know's his name...

Kareem walked back into the kitchen, now in a plain white shirt and dark blue basketball shorts. Arcaida side eyed him, as he sat down to eat. "No, he's not arround." She responded, continuing to stare at Kareem and he raised an eyebrow. "Who on da phone?" He asked, but Arcaida ignored him. "But I am his girlfriend so I can relay the oh so important message." Arcaida said, her stare turning into a glare as Kareem stood up. He was confused as to why she was looking at him like that and why was she not answering his question.

A light chuckle was heard, which only made Arcaida even more mad. What did the bitch think was funny.

"Well this is Malina, you can tell Kareem this scheduled ultra sound for our baby is in two weeks. Have fun playing step mommy lil hoe- Bitch I will beat the dog shit outta you! Do you know who dafuck you talking too?" Arcaida yelled, the fork dropping out of her hand. Whomever this girl may be had her fucked all the way up. This wasnt Dove, that girl was long gone. This is Arcaida and she will beat the shit out of anybody who disrespects her.

So it wasnt the fact that Malina was saying she was preagnant with Kareem's baby, that hadnt even hit her yet, it was the fact that she called Kareem's phone making it seem like she was oh so important then want to call her a hoe? Yea Arcaida finna whoop somebody's ass.

Malina chuckled. If she touched her, she'd be harming Kareem's unborn child of two months.

Kareem had a mug on his face as he tried to take the phone from Arcaida so he could see what was going on, but she kept pushing him back.

"I swea to god on my momma if I eva see you bitch imma stomp the shit outchu. Stomp the shittt outta yo- " Kareem snatched the phone from her and he held it up to his ear as Arcaida paced back and forth.

"Who the fuck is this?" Kareem asked, watching Arcaida pick up the fork and spilled beans and rice. "Hey baby daddy!" Malina said, with a smirk and Kareem instantly knew that voice. "Da fuck is you talking about Malina?" He asked, and Arcaida turned around mugging him. "So you do know dat bitch!" She yelled, and Kareem sighed.

She threw the fork at him. "Speak nigga!" Arcaida yelled, feeling her anger take over her and Kareem raised an eyebrow. "Bye baby daddy, ill see you in two weeks." Malina said, hanging up the phone with a satisfied grin. She didnt know he had a girlfriend but now she could have some fun, while stealing Kareem from her.

"Is dat baby yours?" Arcaida asked, trying to be calm and Kareem placed his phone on the counter with a sigh. "Is da baby yours! Can you not hea no mo my nigga?" Arcaida asked, pushing his head with two fingers and he mugged her. "Back the fuck up Cai. You doing too muc- No You're doing too much!" She cut him off. "You're doing too much!" She repeated continuing to yell and he groaned.

She backed up, swinging her arms back and forth. "Imma ask you one mo damn time." She lowly said and Kareem let out a huff. "Oh my god." He mumbled.

"Is dat dirty bitches baby your- I dont know!" Kareem yelled, standing up straight and holding his arms out. Arcaida was really blowing him and he was already trying to piece together how Malina could be having his baby, then it dawned on him. Those particular seventy two hours, two months ago. He fucked her during some part of that time, and now he fucked up.

"Well I dont know if you got me anymore!" She yelled, with a slight voice crack. Arcaida's mind wasn't even on Malina anymore. It was the fact that her boyfriend has another female preagnant, when they just talked about kids last night. Kareem hates to see her cry and he knew it was coming.

"Cai just lemme tel- Fuck you Kareem." She cut him off, grabbing her phone off the charger and going towards the door. Kareem smacked his lips, grabbing her arm. "Wea is you boutta go!" He yelled, as she continued trying to escape his grip. "None of yo damb business! Ion know everything you do obvious- sly.." Arcaida said, wiping her cheeks from the tears that were falling. Hurt was an understatement...

She finally got out of his grip and she fast walked to the door with him right behind her. "You not even tryna let me explain!" He yelled, as she grabbed a jacket from the hook. "So now you wanna talk?" She said opening the door. "Well ion wanna talk no more." She said, as the door slammed and his fist smashed into the wall.

It was taking everything in him to not go and snatch her up, but he knew that would probably bring back flash backs and he never wanted her to look at him that way. He couldnt let his anger get the best of him.

He looked down at his now bloody fist, before going to the island and grabbing his phone.

Lil Nigga: She witchu right?

Gia mugged her phone, as she listened to her bestfriend whom was in tears.

Ugly ass: Tf is wrong witchu Kareem? Are you dumb? I should come up dere n beatcho stupid ass!

Kareem took that as a sign Arcaida is with her and he clicked his phone off.

"The hell imma do now..." He mumbled, sighing once again.

# Chapter 20

Tears ran down her cheek's as she leaned against the bathroom wall. She felt dumb, but they were indeed tears of joy. She should've known, her moods should have said it all.

The phone rang a couple times before her mother finally picked up. "Ma.." She sobbed, with all her tears falling in the comfort of her mothers conversation. Mae sat up in her bed, at the sound of Arcaida crying. "Cai whats wrong? You ok?" Mae asked, hopping out of bed. Travis rolled over, confused as to where his wife was going. "Wea you goi- Somethings wrong with Cai." Was all she said and Travis hopped up aswell. "Im gone go wake up Cam."

"No ma!" Arcaida yelled, her eyes growing big at the sound of her fathers voice. If he found out her current situation with Kareem he wouldnt be too happy, and Kareems temper is too bad for them to just have a cordial conversation, somebody was gonna end up hurt.

"Wait Travis!" Mae yelled, following her husband but he ignored her. "Now dat you tryna stop me, im really going." He said, shaking Camden and Mae held her head mentally cursing herself out. She rushed back down the hallway, then into the closet in her bedroom. "Are you in some kind of danger? Because if you are im not gonna lie for you, imma let your father handle that but if- Im pregnant ma.." Arcaida sighed, staring at the test.

Mae almost ran out of her room in excitement but the sad tone in Arcaida's caused her to lose her excitement real quick. "You dont sound to happy about that.." Mae noted, and Arcaida felt her tears about to come again. She wanted to talk to her mother about it, but she didnt want to put a bad image of Kareem out there. Fuck it, she doubts they'll ever last now...

"He has another baby momma." She flatly said, wiping the lone tear on her cheek and Mae's smile changed to a sympathetic look. Arcaida has been through a lot of shit, and it seemed like that girl really couldnt catch a break.

"Is the baby his?" Mae asked, lowering her tone once she heard Travis walking by. "He doesnt know...I really didnt give him time to explain. I just wanted to be away from him..." Arcaida admitted and Mae slowly nodded.

"Talk to hi- Momma." Arcaida said, she was scared to even have a conversation with him. One, anything about Malina would piss her off and two, she had never yelled at a man like that in her entire life, so even though it was Kareem she still was scared.

"Arcaida, talk to him." Mae repeated and her daughter sighed. "Fine.." Arcaida shrugged and after they said their goodbyes and I love you's, Mae hung up the phone. "Travis we dont need to go over there, it was something with her period!" Mae yelled, she'll buy Arcaida a little time, but she'll have to handle the rest.

Opening the bathroom door she flinched seeing Kareem stand there, with his expression soft, and still. "Come on Cai dont do that.." He lowly spoke, talking about her flinching in his presence. "I cant help it." She mumbled, looking down at her furry house shoes. "Cai you know I would never hit you right?" He asked, lifting her chin so she could look at him. "Right?' He repeated, confused as to why she was silent, and truthfully she was thinking.

"I know..." She truthfully spoke, at least she did know that. He nodded, letting his hand hang. There was a weird feeling between the two, they both had stuff to say to each other but who was gonna speak first?

Kareem took his eyes off her for a second, and his eyes almost popped out of his head. He reached in the bathroom and grabbed the pregnancy test off the counter, causing Arcaida's heart to beat out of her chest.

"This for real?" He asked, staring down at the positive pregnancy test. "Dont worry about it though, I wont ask for anything, and of course you can see the bab- What the hell are you talking about?" He asked, now mugging her and she crossed her arms.

"I want to break u- No." He cut her off, continuing to mug her. She waved him off. "Its not your decision. Its mine and I dont want to be with you anymore." She lied. There isnt anybody else she want to be with...

"Cai.." Kareem called. All he wanted to do was explain, he doesnt even have time to reflect on him about to be a father because its so much shit going on!

"Kareem please dont make this harder than it should b- Arcaida stop walking away from me and sitcho grown ass down n listen! So wrapped up in whatchu think the truth is, youn wanna hea nobody else!" He yelled, and she slowly turned around, she was startled at first but the rest was just pure shock.

He was tired of playing nice and trying to be cool and collected while she was cussing him out every five seconds.

"Sit down!" He yelled, and she plopped down on the couch, avoiding his gaze. "Stop acting like a child n look at me." He said, now standing in front of her and she cleared her throat. "You dont have to tower over me like da- What?" He asked, not being able to hear her. "You aint gotta stand ova me like dat!" She yelled, now mugging him like he was mugging her.

"Say that then! Sitting over there witcho damn lip poked out!" He yelled back, backing up some and she stood up. "Im not fin- Sitcho ass back on dat mutha fucking couch!" He cut her off and she huffed, plopping back down on the couch. She felt like she was getting bitched, because she is.

He brought one of the chairs from the table over to the living room area, and sitting in front of her. "First of all, that break up shit is dead. You always trying to run from some instead of taking it head on. Stop acting like a punk- You being real disrespectful and im about to slap the shit out you." Arcaida warned, cutting her eyes at him. "I sad sit down and listen, not sit down and talk. You really testing my patience Arcaida." He pointed as he spoke and she rolled her eyes.

"Two, lose that damn attitude." He said, before leaning back in his seat. "Is that al- No, be quiet for five mo minutes at least." He cut her off, just knowing she was about to start yelling and all that again.

"Its sad that I gotta yell at you fo you ta listen. Ion do dat yelling shit no mo, n I try to keep from doing it but you pushing me some wea you wont want me ta be in my head." He explained and she was actually listening.

"Now, two months ago." He started and her jaw tightened. "That day afta dem folk who claimed to be yo peoples came n you kicked me out, I went back to Crato around that time. My sister was going through some shit so I wanted to help ha." He sighed and Arcaida gave him all her attention. "I ended up almost killing him I guess, my mind went blank or some n it felt like I didnt have control of my actions."

"That used to happen to me.." She mumbled, and he nodded. "I see now."

"I went to Malina's house to talk." He started his sentence but was interrupted by Arcaida smacking her lips. "Are you really gone try dat? Talk?" She asked and he plainly looked at her.

"You steady tryna argue n dat shit is annoying. If you woulda really listened you woulda heard the fact that we wasnt together during this time." He explained and she waved him off. "Its the princip- Fuck the principle!" He yelled, shrugging his shoulders.

"Wea was da principle when I gave yo ass chance after chance? Wea was da principle then? Oh school must not have been in session, miss me wit dat shit." He waved her off as he stood.

"Karee- Oh now its Kareem. Das da thing, you want me ta kiss yo ass n apologize for some I did when I wasnt witchu you. Im not boutta do dat nor chase yo ass, so you betta decide whatchu want cause I already know what I want, and das you but if you decide you want me ian finna be yo personal ass kisser, n ian chasing shit but my goals so you betta make a decision quick cause when I stop putting in effort and throw some co parenting shit at you then you gone be hurt." He concluded before looking down at the pregnancy test, that was still in his hand's.

"N ion cae whateva we going through, my kids gone always be straight." He grabbed a paper towel before sitting the test on the counter and walking down the hallway.

He said what he said, it was up to her now.

# Chapter 21

"You good?" Kareem asked, passing Arcaida her bag and she nodded. Even though her head was hurting a little, she had never been on a plane before, she actually never left Mentone.

Kareem observed her face, before nodding and taking her hand into his. Even though Kareem wasnt fond of Malina being one of his kids mother, he was happy about the thought of him being a dad.

Kareem allowed Arcaida to walk in front of him, as they exited the airport. "Dere go my granny." He pointed to his grandmothers Chevrolet Buick GMC and Arcaida smiled, she was excited to actually meet Carol since they only seen each other over facetime.

Arcaida was going to take this little trip as opportunity to meet his family. Even though he's here to go to the Malina's first ultra sound.

Just a few days ago they had another talk, and each of them actually listened to each other. In the end Arcaida chose to make it work, her and Kareem had a new understanding. That being that it was them and only them, but he will always care for his child. Whom has Malina for a mother.

Kareem even mentioned moving to Crato Bay, so he could be able to see his child often. Then the subject of him being in school came up, along with Arcaida's job and her family. Which brought on Kareem to say what about his family. In the end it was another argument made, but they decided they'll choose where they'll live when it comes down to it.

Carol hopped out of the car, with T'suniya and Keyonna following. "Look at da baddest bitch coming to da bay!" T'suniya yelled, giving Arcaida a warm hug as they chuckled. "Hi Cai!" Keyonna yelled, hugging her legs and Arcaida smiled.

"This is amazing! Finally we can meetchu." Carol said, bringing Arcaida into a warm and comforting hug. "It'll be ok." She whispered, rubbing her back and Arcaida's smile only grew.

They pulled back from the hug. "Dont feel preassured to stay with him either, if you feel played then leave." Carol said, not sugar coating nothing. She was disappointed in her grandson, two baby momma's a month apart. Then again, she knew people made mistakes and he's only human.

Marco blew the horn. He had places to be and they was out there having good ol conversation. "Marco blow my damn horn one mo time, imma put yo ass on a plane!" Carol yelled, walking up to the passenger door and everybody chuckled while following.

Kareem wrapped his arm around Arcaida, kissing her forhead. "You good?" He asked, once again and she chuckled. "Im fine Kareem, youn gotta keep asking." She said, as they entered the car. Keyonna had to sit on T'suniya's lap.

"Im just checking luv." Kareem replied, leaning back in the seat, still holding his arm around her and she lied back too, resting her head on his chest.

Thirty minutes into the drive, Carol looked in her rear view seeing Kareem and Arcaida knocked out. She shook her head, making a right off the highway.

"Was on yo mind granny?" Marco asked, seeing her facial expression.

"I feel like something aint right, like some bad finna happen. ." Carol admitted and T'suniya looked at her granny with worry all over her face. "Wea paw paw?" T'suniya asked.

"He's at home. N yall are here wit me, Lauren's at home too..So what is it?" Carol tried to think but nothing was coming to her mind.

Out of the kindness in her heart, of course Carol let Lauren back into her home and this time Lauren kept her word, she finally stopped associating herself with Anthony.

Carol shrugged off the topic, heading towards her home. But she took one more glance in her rear view, feeling that same feeling once again. It was only when she looked at Kareem and Arcaida though.

"Lord be a fence.." Carol mumbled.

Their fifteen minutes away from Carol's house and Kareem and T'suniya kept going back and forth, he had woken up out of his sleep feeling the urge to check on Arcaida. He didnt know what was wrong but this feeling he had told him something bad was about to happen. So, he decided to just stay woke and let her continue to sleep.

"Its the giraffe ass neck fo me." Kareem said, causing Marco to chuckle. "Its the having two baby mommas only a month apart fo me." T'suniya shot back, making a gun with her fingers and rco only laughed louder.

T'suniya slapped the back of his head. "Shut up Lamaont, Thats why Eden ignoring yo down bad ass. Boff of yall is some else." T'suniya said, pointing from Kareem to Marco.

"Marco ova hea playing wit homegirl feelings n you cant keep ya dick in yo pan- T'suniya. I am in the car." Carol said, pulling into her driveway and everybody chuckled, causing Arcaida to sit up while rubbing her eye's. "Ian know I was a pillow." Kareem joked, wiping a eyelash off her cheek and she smiled. "Shit me eitha cause you always laying on me!" She yelled, and everybody started laughing.

Henderick heard doors opening and closing, causing him to stand up from the couch and look out the window. He smiled seeing his family. "Let me go greet dese muthafuckas." He

mumbled, putting Aubrey on the floor, so she could have tum-
my time.

Everyone got out the car except, Carol, T'suniya and Arcaida. T'suniya was waiting for Marco to help Keyonna out of her lap and Carol was texting her husband, telling him and Lauren to come outside. While Arcaida was tying her hair up.

Henderick stepped outside, with a smile on his face. Even though he was happy, he and Kareem were gonna have a talk. A serious one at that. Father hood isn't something to joke or play about, because it's nothing like a father's love.

"Come on Cai." Kareem said, walking away from the car and going towards his paw paw. Henderick dapped him up before pulling him into a hug. "How you feeling Lil nigga?" Henderick asked, and Kareem shrugged. "Good as Imma b- "

Gun shots, signaled Lauren to stand up from her bed and she rushed into the living room only seeing Aubrey but nobody else. She picked her daughter up and knelt down beside a wall, with fear coursing through out her body.

Arcaida's heart beat quickened and her and T'suniya ducked their head down, in the back seat.

When the shots finally stopped, Lauren stood up and grabbed the nearest phone which was her paw paw's and she called the police right away. She didnt know if anybody was hurt, but there was a good chance. It was like the shots were meant for Carol and Henderick's house.

Marco's whole body was in pain, the taste of blood filled his mouth as he looked up to the sky.

Henderick was struggling to move being that he was shot in the leg, but he was trying to get to Marco, he seemed like he was in worse condidtion than Kareem.

Arcaida quickly exited the car, instantly covering her mouth. The body of Carol lied beside the car, with blood all around. She thought she was going to throw up, but instead tears started rolling down her cheeks.

T'suniya helped Keyonna off the ground, being that when Marco got lit up he dropped her out of his arms. Keyonna's cries were loud and when Lauren stepped outside, she felt her heart stop.

Her baby brother, dead. Her grandmother, dead. Her grandfather, injured. Her eldest brother, severely injured and little did she know, it was all because of the man she once loved.

Anthony wasnt just gonna let Kareem beat his ass without any retaliation. But his runners had mistaken Marco for Kareem.....

"K- Kareem! Kareem!" Arcaida yelled, running towards him and it was becoming harder for Kareem to breath by the second.

The ambulance arrived and started to put him on the lift. Arcaida went to get int he ambulance but they wouldn't allow her to.

"Please!" She yelled, and the driver groaned. "The more you resist the less time we have to save him!" He yelled, and she stopped fighting it. She had to be smart in the situation, and what the driver said was true.

Henderick was off in one ambulance and Kareem was in the other. While the Coroners were on their way, so they could get Carol and Marco.

T'suniya's cries mixed with Keyonna's as she held her in her arms. She wouldnt let Keyonna see the dead bodies, it was traumatizing.

Just a few minutes ago, everything was ok. They were laughing and joking...now he's gone..

Her granny, gone...

"Ill drive you to the hospital.." Lauren offered and Arcaida nodded, before they stepped around the bodies getting into the car, along with T'suniya and a still crying Keyonna. She was so young, to experience so much.

Upon getting to the hospital, Kareems phone rang in the seat beside Arcaida. She knew it was Malina and it wasnt the time to be petty, she is having his child too. So, she answered the phone.

"He's at the hospital, Baytiere." Thats all she said, before hanging up the phone. Her cheeks started to sting as the hot tears rolled down her cheeks. "Come on Kareem..." She whispered, holding her hands together. "I need you..."

After arriving at the hospital, of course they weren't told any information and they had to sit there. Now playing the waiting game.

Arcaida tried to keep herself calm, she knew stress wasnt good for pregnant women.

"Where the fuck is my man!" Malina yelled, walking up to Arcaida and she looked up, mugging her. "Bitch get the fuck outta her face!" T'suniya yelled, continuing to hold onto Keyonna's shaking hand.

Lauren mugged Malina. She never liked her, even when Kareem and her were dating in high school. But thats mostly because she thought she was also stealing Kareems attention.

"Get outta my face shawty." Arcaida calmly spoke, as she turned her head to the left. This girl had five seconds to move before she ended up in critical condition. "If I dont?" Malina asked, rubbing her stomach and Arcaida flared her nostrils.

"Ooo! You lucky yo ugly ass is pregnant or I would beatcho ass!" T'suniya yelled, continuing to mug Malina and Malina waved her off. "So you aborting dat baby right?" She asked. and Arcadia looked up at her with a raised eyebrow as Lauren's jaw dropped.

"Whatchu say?" Arcaida asked, standing up and Malina backed up a little, but she tried to play it off like she wasnt scared. "Matta fact, I said I was gone beatcho ass n I meant it!" Arcaida yelled, punching Malina right in her mouth. "Damn!" T'suinya yelled.

Just because she was pregnant didnt means he couldnt hit her face. "Ion cae if you having his child, whatchu not gone do is disrespect me!" Arcaida yelled as Malina stood there, holding her mouth which was in excruciating pain.

Arcaida bumped past her, going towards the double door's. She needed some air.

Just wait until these baby's drop, Malina is in for a good ass beating. Until then, Arcaida was only worried about two people.

Her grandfather and the love of her life...

# Chapter 22

"Thirteen years ago today, Crato Bay's top criminal Anthony Richmond was arrested and sentenced life after a shooting that resulted in the deaths of sixty year old Car- "

The channel was changed, being that Arcaida heard footsteps coming her way.

A pair of strong arms, wrapped around her waist and she smiled looking up at her husband. He pecked her lips, growing a smile of his own.

"Whatchu doing in hea by yoself?" Kareem asked, letting her go and sitting on their king sized bed. "Nothing." Arcaida responded, before going to look in the mirror. "How you feeling?" She asked, looking at him through the mirror as she removed her hair tie, letting her locs hang and they moved freely near her elbows.

"Beleive it or not, im actually good this year." Kareem truthfully spoke. He'd usually get down and sad around this time but this year, he was ok...

Arcaida nodded. "Well, come on." She said, turning around and holding her hand out, Kareem once again smiled taking hold of his wife's hand and following her out of their bedroom. They walked down the hallway, decorated with pictures of the Jacksons and Jhonsons, even some together.

The sound of music and conversation became louder and louder, as they went towards the kitchen.

"Dea she go..ask her." Elijah said, pointing to his auntie Cai and Marco chuckled. "You a bitch boy." He said, mushing Elijah's head and Rayne chuckled, along with Kaniya.

"Just go ask." Elijah said, pointing again and Marco smacked his lips, before standing up from the couch and walking towards in the kitchen, where all the grown folks were. "Ma." Marco called, trying to get his mothers attention but she was too busy laughing with his auntie Lauren to pay him any attention. "Momma!" He called again, and Arcaida smacked her lips, looking down at him. "What Mj?" She asked. "Can Elijah stay da night?" Marco asked and Arcaida nodded. "I dont care if his momma dont care."

Marco smiled before rushing back over to his cousin and sisters. "My momma said if auntie Gia let you stay den you can stay." Marco said, plopping down on the couch and Elijah nodded. "Im boutta go ask my momma den." He said, standing up and everybody nodded.

"Ma! Wea you at?" Elijah yelled, and Gia walked in from the back door, with her fiancé. "What boy? Yelling like dat, just embarrassing." She said, placing her wine cooler on Kareem and Arcaida's marbled island counter.

Over the years a lot has changed, and everyone has something different going on. Kareem, he's a personal trainer and he also has his own studio. Arcaida's now the owner of a few of her own restaurants and the one her mother started her off at thirteen years ago. Gia's a fashion desginer, a well known one at that and her fiancé Storm works right beside her.

Lauren finally got her life together and went to college, now she's a doctor, one of the best in Crato Bay. T'suniya own's her own little boutique where Gia designs some of the clothes she sell's. Keyonna is a modal, and she walks the run way in the clothes Gia designs.

"Can I stay over hea?" Elijah asked, as Gia kept messing with his hair. "Yea n dont be stressing yo auntie n uncle out eitha." She warned, before mushing his head and Elijah chuckled before walking back over to his cousins. "Guess who staying here tongiht?" He yelled, holding his arms out and the girls got hyped. "You!" They yelled, and all of them started laughing.

"Yall so lame." Aubrey said, walking in from the back door and Camden, and Keyonna came in right behind her. "Girlll fuck you." Kaniya said, chuckling a little bit and Marco smiled, giving his baby sister a high five. He taught her that.

"Im finna snitch on yo lil ass." Camden said, pointing at Kaniya and she smacked her lips. "Dont be a bitch boy." Elijah said, mugging Camden and Keyonna couldnt hold her laugh's anymore. She was cracking up.

These kids was bad as hell when unsupervised.

"Rayne you staying hea tonight or you going to yo mommas?" Marco asked, and everybody looked her way. "Ion know, dad said I could stay if I wanted too but yall know how my momma be. Dont wanna neva let me go no wea." Rayne rolled her eyes, at the thought of her jealous ass momma.

"Yo momma stay bitchin- Shut up." Keyonna slapped Camden's shoulder. He didnt need to be bath mouthing that girl's momma like that, especially in front of her.

"My fault." Camden apologized, before checking his messages. Camden is currently in college, playing basketball and football along with running track. Kareem had taught him how to play basketball and his father taught him how to play football.

"Ooo. I gotta lil date to get to." He smirked, standing up straight and Aubrey gagged, causing him to throw one of the decorative pillows at her and they chuckled. "Unt unt! We not fucking up my house dis year!" Arcaida yelled, pointing at them and all the kids groaned. They mess her house up every year and she'd left to clean it. Not this time.

"Fuck yall groaning fo?" Kareem asked, with a raised eyebrow and everybody got quiet. "Mhm." He hummed before turning back to his grandfather, father n law, and his two bestfriends Rod and Piere.

Rod and Piere have been Kareem's friends since he started living with his grandmother. They welcomed him to the block, showed him around, and was just accepting.

"Hollon cause my brother said, Back talk!" Keyonna yelled and T'suniya chuckled. "Its quiet aint no back talk!" She finished and everybody started laughing, including Kareem.

The sound of the front door opening caught everybody's attention and in walked Eden, whom had a smal smile on her face. "Hey everybody!" She waved and they all smiled, waving back.

"Nelly say hey den go play witcho cousins." Eden said, looking down at Penelope and she waved. "Hi everybody!" Penelop spoke before looking back to her momma. "Can I go now?" She asked and Eden nodded, watching her run into the living room.

"Wassup bitches!" Penelope greeted her cousins and they chuckled. "Why is dese kids so bad!" Aubrey asked, and Keyonna was on the floor laughing. "Ion know but im finna be out." Camden said, before dapping Elijah and Marco up, then heading towards Kareem and nem.

"Ay im outta hea!" Camden said, catching Kareem's attention. "Wea yo lil ass boutta go?" Travis asked and Camden turned around pointing to Keyonna. "Tell em Kee!" He yelled, before heading towards Arcaida and giving her a quick hug, then kisisng his mommma on the cheek before heading towards the door.

"My brotha said, you in his business!" Keyonna yelled, sitting up. "Do- Dont do dat!" Rayne, Kaniya and Penelope finished the line, at the same time and everybody chuckled.

"Caii!" Eden yelled, and Arcaida chuckled, placing her wine cooler on the counter before embracing Eden in a warm and comforting hug. "How you feeling?" Arcaida asked and Eden nodded, putting on a brave face. "Im good as im gone get." she responded and Arcaida nodded. "Nelly looked like every bit of Marco. Just the girl version." She thought out loud and Eden nodded.

When Eden found out Marco was dead, she was filled with regret. One, she had been ignoring him that whole day. Two day's before that, her and Marco had spent that whole day together. Just enjoying each other's company and at the end of that day, she willingly lost her virginity. But, the next morning she asked him were they something serious, something she knew she should have asked the night before but she didnt.

Marco told her the plain truth, that he didnt think he'd be able to treat her right. He felt like he'd end up fucking over her and that pissed Eden off. He shouldn't have had sex with her in that case. Now, she wishes she would have answered the phone, but she has Penelope. That little girl will always remind her of her first love.

Kareem looked around at his family, these are his people and he couldnt see life without them. "You ok?" Arcaida asked, coming up beside her husband and Kareem smiled, placing his beer on the counter and bringing her into his arms.

"You wanna know some." He asked and Arcaida nodded, looking into his eyes. "You are a large part of my world that I never thought I'd have. I look at life differently, and in the way I see it some people may find it hard to bare, but now with my Tender Soul I appreciate life more." He lowly spoke, and with a big smile on her face, she layed her head on his chest as Erykah Badu - Next Lifetime, played over the speaker's and she sang to him as they slow danced in their kitchen.

Soon everybody was gathered in the kitchen, including the kids. They all listened to Arcaida's beautiful voice while watching the lovely couple dance.

It was a true tender moment...

www.ingramcontent.com/pod-product-compliance
Lightning Source LLC
Chambersburg PA
CBHW071018180726
48291CB00004B/1516